The Fall Of Emrys

By Ian T. Wilson

Ian Wilson
2022

First Printing: 2022

ISBN: 979-8-9866880-0-8
Ian T. Wilson 46 Edward st.Malone, New York, 12953
Ianthomaswilson.com

Pronunciation guide

Taliesin: tale-YES-in

Gwion: g-WEE-on

Gwyn: g-WIN

Creirwy: CREER-wee

Emrys Wledig: EM-ris LED-dig

Uther: OO-thur

Crom Cruach: Crom cROO-akh

Ceridwen: CARE-id-when

Tegid: TEG-id

Nimue: NIM-weh

Llyr: LEER

Domhnall: DON-all

Connall: CON-all

Kynyr: kin-NOOR

Annwyn: AN-new-win

Igerna: ee-GURN-ah

Gorlois: gor-LO-is

Oengus: ON-gus

Odarnat: o-Dar-nat

Eithne: ETH-knee

Fionnlagh: FIN-law

Prologue

It was a pub, a typically British pub, with a Union Jack hanging above the bar. As this was in the days before electricity was widely available in England, kerosene lamps filled the pub with a friendly yellow light. A roaring fire warmed the air about the jolly patrons on that cold winter night. Men sang folk songs to the merry sound of the fiddle.

A fair-haired, bearded man sat at the far end of the bar, puffing thoughtfully on his pipe and occasionally sipping his brew. He appeared to be a man of late-middle age, but had a strange youthful twinkle in his blue-gray eyes, clothed in a dark blue pullover, with gray trousers and well-worn brown boots. He was a regular at this pub, or a semi-regular, as he would often disappear for weeks or months at a time. Sometimes the townsfolk thought him dead, but then he would suddenly return as if from the grave.

The serving girl, a young woman of about eighteen or twenty years of age, approached him, staring intently at him through clear gray eyes. She reminded the man of someone else he had known with those same gray eyes many, many years before. Surely, she carried the blood of kings in her veins.

"Can I get you anything else, Mr. Elwyn?" she asked.

"Oh, thank you, Miss Bowen, but I'm quite satisfied," replied the gentleman.

"At least allow me to refill your cup," she replied.

"Well, alright. Another beer will do me no harm."

Taking Mr. Elwyn's cup, the serving girl refilled it and passed it back to him.

"Now," said the gentleman. "I suppose there's something you want in exchange for this."

"Whatever do you mean?" asked Miss Bowen, feigning ignorance.

"You've been eyeing me all evening, bringing me one drink after another without my even asking for it. Now, I suppose you wish to hear another tale of King Emrys."

The girl chuckled a bit, brushing her curly dark hair away from her blushing cheek.

"If you would be so kind, Mr. Elwyn."

Elwyn smiled. "If you insist."

The girl leaned in to hear the man over the din of patrons as Elwyn began his tale.

-1-

The crow of a rooster announced the dawn of a new day in Camelot, rousing me from my slumber on that fair morning in Spring. I was in good spirits that day, drinking in the cool, sweet air filtering through the window. Inching closer to my wife, Creirwy, I drew back the raven-black curtain of her hair and caressed her fair cheek with a kiss.

"Good morning, beautiful," I said, barely above a whisper.

"Not now, Gwion!" she mumbled.

"My love, it is sunrise on the first of May."

"Ugh, why must the sun rise so early?" she moaned, drawing the covers over her tousled head.

I smiled at her reluctance to rise from bed. "Because that is the way of things, dear."

"Go get your lyre and sing it back to sleep for an hour."

"There are some spells even I cannot perform, my dear," I said with a laugh. "Now, let us rise and bring in the summer!"

"Fine," she sighed, throwing off the covers. Goose-pimples arose on her skin as it met the cold air.

Gingerly, she stepped over to the chest where we kept our clothes and drew out the garments she intended to wear that day. I sat at the edge of the bed, admiring her beauty as she dressed. I was often struck by how fortunate I was to have such a lovely wife as Creirwy.

"Goodness, my hair is a fright!" said she, looking into a small hand mirror.

I chuckled. "You are lovely no matter what your hair looks like."

"Still, I cannot go out on May Day looking like a crow's nest," she replied, aggressively combing her hair into submission. "Enough lounging about, Gwion! Get dressed! We have a long day ahead of us!"

She tossed a tunic at me, which landed squarely on my face. With a hearty laugh, I shoved the garment over my head. A moment ago, I could barely convince her to get out of bed; now it seemed she could not wait to begin the festivities of the day.

May Day was a high day then, much as it is now in many places; a day of dancing and singing and feasting. Our tradition was to have Father Dubric and myself bless the fields, much as I had done as a boy in Ceredigion. Creirwy would be accompanying us for the first time, and I was greatly looking forward to celebrating the festival with her at my side.

Once we had dressed, we left our room in the great house of the king and went to the outer courtyard on our way to the church for morning prayers. Standing in the courtyard were the High King Emrys, Nimue his queen, and his brother, Uther. With them were Lord Gorlois of Kernow and his wife, Igerna, and their two small daughters, Morgana and Morgause. All appeared to be waiting on Creirwy and I.

"Taliesin," said Emrys with a smile. "We were beginning to wonder if you would be joining us."

"Good morrow, your majesty," I said. "Forgive my tardiness."

"It was my fault," said Creirwy. "My hair, you know."

The queen laughed. "Perfectly understandable."

"Good morning, Taliesin and Creirwy," said Morgana with a smile. "I made this for you."

She handed Creirwy a garland of wildflowers.

"Oh, it's lovely, Morgana, thank you!" my wife replied, placing the garland on her head.

"Well, let us not tarry any longer," said Lord Uther. "To the church!"

We walked in a quiet procession through the streets of Camelot toward the church, peasants and court officials joining us along the way. King Emrys was not a lover of pomp and required no retinue to accompany him. He trusted his subjects as his subjects trusted him. He did not fear them at all; he was beloved by most, and all feared Caledbur, his ancient and powerful blade.

Thus we entered the church reverently as the liturgy began. As the prayers were said and the Scriptures read, I will confess that my mind wandered to other things. Despite the joy of this day, my thoughts turned to darker things. Visions of death had filled my mind in the night. I had a sense that King Emrys' doom was imminent, though I could not say why.

Once the prayers and scripture had concluded, the festivities began. As the parish priest, it was Father Dubric's duty to lead the procession. His thurible swung back and forth as we processed through the city streets and out of the great timber gates to the countryside. Creirwy and I walked directly behind him, leading the May song while the royal family followed behind us, along with various and sundry revelers.

Out we went, singing and dancing down the meandering paths through the homesteads as Dubric and I blessed the fields, wishing the karls a fruitful season. Karls, if you remember from my previous tales, work the land under the protection of the king.

The karls and their families met our party with great joy as they did every year, inviting Dubric to bless their animals and children as well as their crops. Despite her dour mood earlier that morning, Creirwy was in high spirits, singing the May song as fervently as I did, dancing gracefully about the field, weaving her magic into her words. Everywhere her bare feet trod, wildflowers sprang up.

After a long day of dancing and singing, we made our way back to the city, where the citizens had prepared a great feast. Huge tables laden with food and drink stood in the town square. A great shout arose from the crowds as we returned, and immediately, we sat down to feast. We ate, we drank, we sang, we danced; it was quite a merry time for all.

Exhausted from my labors, I reclined drowsily at the table, Creirwy sitting beside me, feeding me strawberries. Morgana and Morgause lay by the wall, fallen asleep as children who have been playing all day often do. Uther and Gorlois discussed hunting exploits while Igerna listened attentively, occasionally commenting on her husband's exaggerations. Across from us sat Emrys and Nimue. The queen's eyelids drooped as she laid her head against the king's broad chest.

"Are you happy, wife?" asked Emrys, stroking her dark hair with great affection.

"How could I not be, with this much mead and a husband as handsome and strong as yourself?" responded Nimue. "The question is, dear husband, are *you* happy?"

"I am brimming with joy, dear wife. More than that, I am brimming with desire."

"Desire for what?" asked Nimue.

"I can hold our secret in no longer."

The queen lifted her head and looked directly into Emrys' gray eyes. "Then say on, my king."

With a hearty laugh, Emrys crushed the elf maid to his chest and kissed her passionately. Rising from his seat, the king raised a toast.

"People of Camelot, my friends. I have an announcement to make: there will soon be another to carry on my name. Queen Nimue is with child!"

The people cheered.

"Long live the queen!" said Emrys, draining his cup.

Leaping up, Creirwy embraced the queen joyfully.

"Oh that's wonderful, Queen Nimue! I am so happy for you!" she said.

"Thank you, Creirwy. I am indeed blessed beyond measure."

"You will make a wonderful mother," added Igerna.

"Congratulations, your kingship!" said a familiar voice.

Peering through the crowd, I beheld the grinning faces of Domhnall and Conall McCallum, the Gaelic fishermen who accompanied me on my last adventure.

My lips curved into a smile as I went to meet the two Hibernians.

"Domhnall! Conall! It is Good to see you again. What brings you to Camelot?"

"Well, if we'd known there'd be this much free beer and food, we'd have come sooner!" said Conall with a laugh.

"Verily," I replied. "May Day is one of the high days of the year in Camelot."

"Greetings," said the king to the two fishermen. "I believe we've met before."

"That we did," responded Domhnall. "We helped your bard and his lady there out of a wee scrape some months ago."

"I suppose you are here to trade, or perhaps gamble and lose money, forcing you to steal away in the dead of night," quipped Creirwy.

Conall laughed heartily. "Not this time. We've come on something of an errand of mercy, actually."

"Oh yes?" asked King Emrys

"Aye. It concerns you, actually," said Domhnall. "We have a message from Bishop Patrick."

The fisherman drew a small scroll from his purse and handed it to the king. Opening the scroll Emrys read it carefully, a look of deep concern washing over his face.

"What is it, my love?" asked Nimue.

"Apparently the whole of Hibernia is overrun with werewolves; the servants of the black god, Crom Cruach."

A chill ran down my spine. Crom Cruach was one of the most feared of all the old gods. He was a mysterious, aloof deity, living in the dark forests of Hibernia, lusting after the blood of mortal children. Some said he was a great black wolf. Others said he resembled a man clothed in black. Many said he was a shape-shifter. One thing they all agreed upon; he was not to be trifled with.

The king grew pale. It was no idle matter to challenge Crom. Tales of his savagery had reached all across the Western world.

"We shall have a formal council on it in the morrow," he said at last. "We have all had much wine, and such decisions must be made with a clear mind."

"Of course," said Domhnall.

News of such gravity had darkened the King's mood, as well as mine. We sat silent and sober, despite all the joy and levity about us.

About midnight, the revelers returned to their respective abodes, as did Creirwy and I.

"What do you suppose King Emrys will do?" asked Creirwy as she undid the fastenings on her gown.

"Render aid to the Hibernians, I suppose," I responded, leaning down to untie my sandals.

"Well, obviously!" retorted Creirwy. "But Crom is one of the most powerful of the old gods. He will not be easy to defeat."

"True," I agreed.

"What I am saying is that I do not fancy you going on a long and dangerous campaign in Hibernia."

"Neither do I; least of all, being away from that lovely face for any length of time."

Creirwy wrapped her slender arms about my neck.

"They say absence sharpens love."

"Aye, though I cannot imagine my love being much sharper."

Creirwy pressed her warm lips to mine.

"Come to bed," I said. "We will think about Hibernia in the morning."

King Emrys took his seat upon the throne in the great hall of Camelot, his queen by his right hand, Uther at his left. I of course was there, as well as Lord Gorlois, Father Dubric and Menuu the magician in places of lesser honor, with earls and barons and proconsuls.

The Hibernians knelt before the king as they entered the council chamber.

"Arise, Conall and Domhnall McCallum," said Emrys. "State your case before the council."

"Well, your lordships," began Conall. "There's been a spot of bother with the werewolves."

"The country is overrun with them, you see," added Domhnall. "Crom Cruach has set them upon the land and Bishop Patrick is having a devil of a time expelling them. We came here to ask for your aid."

"See, he's of the opinion that only the sword Caledbur, which you yourself possess, is able to slay Crom," stated Conall. "I figured it wouldn't hurt to ask you to pop over to Hibernia and kill a god for us."

Emrys scratched his square jaw.

"So the question before us is should we help Hibernia?" inquired Uther.

"That's about the size of it, your impressive-ness," responded Conall.

"Well, that is not much of a question, is it?" remarked Nimue. "We cannot leave the Hibernians to be assailed in such a savage manner."

"Besides," added Uther, "the more innocent blood he spills, the stronger he grows. If the gods gain strength, they shall soon be upon our doorstep again."

"This may be true," I said, "however, I fear it may be some sort of trick of Tegid or Ceridwen; distract you in Hibernia while they attack the kingdom. Besides, you have Nimue and your child to consider."

The king nodded. "This is all true, Taliesin. What say you, Gorlois?"

Lord Gorlois was a quiet man; he spoke little unless he was directly asked, but he had proven himself to be a man of peculiar insight.

"While I agree that this evil must be eradicated," he stated, "we cannot leave the kingdom unprotected."

"I have a proposal," said Menuu.

"Say on, magician," replied Emrys. By the tone of his voice, I could tell that he did not truly care what Menuu had to say; he and Menuu did not always see eye-to-eye, and he often wondered why Uther kept the magician around. Still, he had to listen to all voices.

"You split your forces," continued Menuu. "Send a delegation to Hibernia with Uther and stay here yourself with your main forces."

The king paused for a moment.

"A rather wise plan, I would say," said Uther.

I nodded in agreement. "Uther is a capable warrior and strategist. He will bring us victory."

"Very well," said Emrys at last. "We split our forces. Uther shall lead a delegation of men to Hibernia while I remain in Camelot. Taliesin, you shall accompany them to record the tale."

"As you wish, good king," I replied.

I did not like the idea of leaving King Emrys here, not because I feared Crom, but because I feared that without my guidance, the king might fall into some peril. By this time, I had been troubled by many visions of King Emrys' doom. While I had discussed these visions with Emrys, he had simply chosen to continue living as he always had, and let events happen as they might. This encapsulated his whole philosophy; He would continue doing what seemed good and right, and accept whatever happened as a result.

"I shall stay here by your side until they return, good king," said Gorlois. "I have a strange feeling you will be needing me."

I breathed a sigh of relief; at least he would have the wisdom of Gorlois to help him.

"Splendid!" exclaimed Conall. "When do we leave?"

"It should take us two days to assemble a proper war band and prepare the ships," said Uther.

"Let us make no delay then," said King Emrys.

...

Back and forth I paced, placing some belongings into a bag, making ready for the journey I would be embarking on in a few days time. Creirwy helped me by placing a few items which I had not thought that I needed. Creirwy was a practical woman; always thinking of the things which frequently slipped my mind.

"I do not think you need worry yourself about the king," she said, placing an extra pair of stockings into the bag. "He can protect himself. And he has Nimue to help him."

"And you, of course," I replied.

"Me?" exclaimed Creirwy, "Why, I am going with you!"

"Creirwy, darling, it is too dangerous for you to go to Hibernia."

"We faced a conqueror wyrm, we fought Llyr the sea god, my own mother is Ceridwen, the queen of darkness and you think Hibernia is too dangerous?"

We glared at one another for a span.

"Fine," I said at last, "You raise a good point, but I need you to stay here and watch over the king."

"Very well," Creirwy huffed. "But I will not enjoy one moment of it!"

"I would expect nothing less, my dear," I said, and kissed her tenderly.

...

The mid-morning air echoed with the cries of gulls as we assembled on the wharf. Father Dubric moved down the lines of men preparing to depart, blessing us with holy oil. The ship of war floated in the bay, waiting to be filled with some of Britain's finest men.

"We shall return victorious," said Uther.

"I shall see to that," replied King Emrys.

Unbuckling his sword belt, the king approached Uther and looped it about his waist. "It is in good hands. I know you will use it rightly."

Uther nodded. "I shall endeavor to do so, brother."

The royal brothers embraced one last time before Uther stepped onto the gangplank. Tears rolled down Creirwy's fair face as she approached me. For once she said nothing at all, only throwing her arms about me and pressing her lips into mine.

"I will return," I said.

"You had better," she replied, wiping the tears from her eyes.

With that, the rest of the men got into the ship, and Uther gave the order to depart. The oarsmen grunted as they rowed us out of the Estuary into the frothing sea.

On the second day, we arrived at the port of Corcach in the southern part of Hibernia. Into the broad harbor, where there were many ships moored, we sailed. The Hibernians stared in astonishment at the great British battleship with Lord Uther at the prow. Surely, they had rarely seen such a grand sight as this.

The McCallum brothers rowed into one of the docks and tied up their fishing boat as Uther and his men followed.

"Welcome to Hibernia, your lordship!" cried Conall in a clear voice.

The men filed onto the alien shore, greeted by the quizzical expressions of the natives.

Conall, with his usual charm, greeted them warmly. I wonder if there was any spot in all the Western World where he had not made friends, or enemies, for that matter.

"Follow me," said the fisherman. "I'll take you to meet King Oengus."

King Oengus, I later learned, was the default high king of Hibernia, though no one could truly claim such a title. The other kings simply deferred to him as their chief. He was the man to speak to on any matter involving the nation of Hibernia.

We followed the fishermen through winding gravel streets of Corcach. The town was rustic, much like many other towns of the Gaels. It was not so much a town in the British or Roman sense as it was a large grouping of round houses with conical thatched roofs. Some of the houses were of timber, few were stone, most were made of cobb; some were large, others were small. Sheep, goats, cattle and swine wandered about the place. Dogs ran back and forth, playing and baying at one another and the half-naked children playing in the streets. Peasants went back and forth, going about their daily duties. Many paused to observe the fighting men of Britain.

The people of Hibernia were a hardy, handsome race. Most were tall, with freckled, ruddy skin; many had red hair, though brown or gold were also common. In those days, Gaelic men were typically beardless, shaving all parts of their faces with the exception of the upper lip, from which they grew bushy mustaches. They often cut the hair of the sides of their heads, allowing it to grow long on top. The women usually wore their hair long and loose, falling from their heads in waves and curls.

Their mode of dress was similar to many in the Northern world at that time: men usually wore trousers and tunics, while women usually wore long gowns. Tartan fabric was common, as evidenced by the displays of colorful patterned fabric adorning all who dwelt there.

Suddenly, there came the sound of a large brass horn. Out of the crowds marched a war-host, led by a strong Gaelic warrior. A tartan cloak hung about his broad shoulders, fastened by a gold brooch. His gold torc, rings, armlets, and bracelets identified him as a king. A red-brown mane cascaded down to his shoulders from under an ornate, horned helm. His whiskered face hardened like granite.

"King Oengus," said Conall.

"Your majesty," added Domhnall.

I had a feeling this was another in a long line of men who had been cheated or humiliated by Conall.

"Horse thieves," grumbled the king.

"We won fair and square and you know it," retorted Domhnall.

The three men stared at one another for a few tense moments, like wolves squaring off. It seemed like the whole world grew silent, waiting for one of them to make the first move. Out of the corner of my eye, I saw Uther's hand edging toward his sword. I too rested my hand on my blade; if there was to be bloodshed, I would rather die fighting. At last, they burst into uncontrollable laughter before embracing one another.

"It's good to see you two again, sea dogs!" said the king.

"I was beginning to wonder if we'd be welcomed in the realm of Mhumhain again, after our last game of dice," said Domhnall.

"Water under the bridge," replied the king. "I've heard some rumors going around that you'd finally settled down with a good woman, Conall. That can't be accurate, can it?"

"Indeed it is!" replied Conall.

"If I didn't hear it with me own ears, I wouldn't have believed it! Conall McCallum? Settling down? Bah!"

"It took a bit of convincing," said Domhnall.

This whole exchange was spoken in the Hibernian tongue, of which Uther understood not one word, but I spoke with perfect fluency - one of the benefits I gained having drunk of the brew of wisdom as a child.

"Now, who are these fine gents with you?" asked the king.

"This is Lord Uther Pendragon of Camelot and his host," replied Domnall, "They're here to help with your werewolf problem."

The king's countenance darkened.

"What, by the ancestors, makes you think we need *their* help?" Oengus snapped.

"Surely not the devil, King Oengus," said a voice, also speaking Gaelic.

The crowds parted reverently before a man in clerical garb. He had a kindly demeanor, yet I sensed an air of authority. I came to the conclusion that this was none other than Patrick, the enlightener of Hibernia. With him walked a monastic, his hood drawn over his head so that I could not see his face, but he had a peculiar, hobbling gait which struck a chord of familiarity.

"Bishop Patrick, I presume," said Uther in his native Cumbric.

"It is I," replied the bishop, also in Cumbric. "And you are King Emrys Wledig?"

"Nay, Reverend Father," replied Uther. "The king has remained at Camelot. I am Uther, Emrys' brother. I have been sent to act in his stead."

"Germanus spoke very highly of you both," replied the bishop.

"And I have heard a good report of you, Reverend."

"Now that we're all acquainted," interjected Domhnall, "mind helping me keep Oengus from kicking his lordship off the bloody island?"

Patrick sighed and spoke in Gaelic. "King Oengus, be reasonable. Crom is far beyond our ability to defeat."

"You preach every day about the power of God and how He can deliver those who call upon Him," barked Oengus, "why not pray to Him to deliver us from this plague?"

"God often works through men to perform his will," replied Patrick. "Perhaps Uther *is* our deliverance."

Oengus glared at us. "You have come a long way," he said at last. "T'would be bad form to turn you away now. Come: to my fortress. I'll give you some food and place to spend the night."

"What was all that about?" inquired Uther.

"Oh, Oengus isn't keen on outsiders involving themselves in his affairs," replied Conall. "Been that way since we were wee lads."

"He will come around, I am sure," said Bishop Patrick.

King Oengus led us to a stone wall enclosing a grouping of round stone houses. This was his fortress. Within the wall, an enormous Hibernian hound greeted the king enthusiastically. She was a tall beast, but thick boned, with muscles like cords. About her neck and chest was a leather harness studded with long iron spikes. Oengus vigorously ruffled the shaggy brown fur of the animal, who then proceeded to inspect us with an air of suspicion.

"Hullo there, Odarnat!" said Conall to the hound. "Good to see you, lass!"

The hound seemed to take a liking to me. She looked deeply into my eyes with an almost human expression. I almost wondered if she possessed a rational soul, but such an idea seemed preposterous at the time.

We entered the largest of the houses, where Oengus directed us to sit on low benches as servants prepared supper for us.

Into the great house stepped a young woman. Long, silvery hair fell nearly to her hips. Her eyes were as blue as a winter sky. She wore a blue-gray gown after the custom of Gaelic women; a tartan shawl hung about her shoulders. In her left hand was a harp of Hibernian make, in her right was a long staff. She repeatedly tapped on the ground ahead of her in such a way that I deduced that she was blind.

"Ah, Fionnlagh," said King Oengus. "We have esteemed guests; Lord Uther of Camelot, his war band and his bard, Taliesin."

"The prince of bards?" exclaimed Fionnlagh.

"The very same!" replied Domhnall.

An expression of delight crossed the young woman's face. "Where is he?" she inquired.

"Here!" I replied, rising up to meet her.

The woman walked toward me, tapping with her staff. The monk who had accompanied Patrick earlier that day hobbled toward her.

"Here, Fionnlagh, let me help you," said the monk as he attempted to guide her toward me. There was something about his voice that nagged at my memory, but I could not place it.

"It's alright, Afagdu, I can manage," said Fionnlagh.

My blood ran cold. Afagdu, son of Tegid. He had tried to murder me on two occasions, the second of which I let him go free. Afagdu's life had been pain and misery from the very start. Conceived by Tegid's ungodly sorcery, the lad had been born deformed, thus his odd gate and grotesque features which he concealed under the monk's hood.

"Afagdu?" I exclaimed.

The son of Tegid drew back his hood, revealing his ape-like face.

"You know one another?" asked Fionnlagh.

"Yes," I replied. "He was my foster-brother, once upon a time."

"Oh really. Was that when you lived in Ceredigion?"

"Nay; before that, when we lived in Bala."

Fionnlagh drew in her breath. "This isn't a tale I've heard."

"It is not a tale I like to tell," I replied. "How came you here, Afagdu?"

"After you set me free, I wandered aimlessly, begging and stealing for my bread, sleeping wherever I could find shelter. I came to the conclusion eventually that my life had no purpose and sought to end it. As I was about to throw myself from a cliff into the raging sea, some holy men stopped me and asked why I was trying to end my life. I told them my story and they invited me to eat supper with them. We talked for a long time. Then they invited me to come to Hibernia with them, which is where I met Patrick. I had never heard anyone speak like him, with such authority. Now I serve the highest God."

"That is a remarkable story," I responded once his tale had concluded.

Afagdu looked at me with a crooked smile and said: "Truly, I have found the peace I sought."

"He is indeed a fervent youth," interjected Patrick. "He will make a good monk, should he choose to make his final vows."

"Thank you, Reverend Father," replied Afagdu.

"Talking of stories," said Fionnlagh, "I would like to hear some of yours, Taliesin. Is it true that your songs defeated the great dragon of the north seas?"

"It is," I responded with a smile.

"I saw with me own eyes!" added Conall.

"So you've said, Conall," said Fionnlagh, "but I know your gift for embellishment."

Domhnall and Oengus burst into raucous laughter.

"How long will you be in Hibernia?" queried Fionnlagh.

"Until Crom Cruach is defeated," I replied.

Fionnlagh's eyebrows shot up. "Crom Cruach?"

"That is why we have come," I responded. "To kill Crom and his host of wolfmen."

"There will be time to speak of that later," said Oengus. "Refresh yourselves first."

The servants brought forth meat, fish, vegetables, and mead, serving them to us on heaping platters. It was a fine feast indeed. King Oengus and the McCallum brothers spoke of their various adventures since the last time they had met, Conall exaggerating details in his usual manner.

"Then Llyr himself came out!" said Conall. "He must've been nine ells tall!"

"Conall, it is a sin to lie," interjected Patrick.

"Oh, come on, Patrick!" responded Conall. "It's just a wee bit of exaggeration."

The bishop rolled his eyes as the fisherman continued his tale.

Uther said almost nothing during the meal, as Oengus did not speak Cumbric, and Uther thought it uncouth to speak in a language his host did not comprehend.

"We have heard nothing of the exploits of Lord Uther," remarked King Oengus. Once again, I acted as translator for Lord Uther, conveying the Hibernian's words to him in Cumbric.

"I am not much of a teller of tales," said Uther. "Taliesin is much more gifted in that art than I; he would be better suited to the task."

I could not but oblige. Placing my lyre on my lap, I sang a song of the battle of Camelot, in which Uther fought bravely. Though I had never sung in Hibernian up to that point in time, the words flowed freely through me as though I had been born on the Emerald Isle.

There was a long, awestruck silence after my song concluded. King Oengus wiped away tears of joy and said: "Prince of bards indeed. How came you to know the tongue of the Gaels? You sing it like a true Hibernian."

"I know many tongues of men by the virtue of the brew of wisdom," I replied.

"That is another tale I'd like to hear."

As I was about to begin the story of how I drank of a draught of the magical brew of Ceridwen, there was a sudden, blood-curdling howl, followed shortly thereafter by another. A look of terror overtook the faces of the Hibernians.

"He's here," said Patrick.

"To arms!" ordered the king.

Oengus and his men immediately arose from the table, rushing to the armory to outfit themselves for battle. Uther, not to be outdone, readied for the fight, his men following him into the night. I of course came with the company to record the battle and offer whatever assistance I might.

"Stay here, Fionnlagh," said Afagdu. "It's too dangerous out there."

"I want to help!"

"You can help by offering prayer for us," said Patrick as he led us out into the dark, bold as a lion.

Out into the charnel blackness I went, lyre in hand, my heart beating like a drum in my chest. The whole town was in an uproar, the cries of men, women and children mixed with the howls of the werewolves in a discordant choir of madness. One of the powers granted to me by my draught of the brew of wisdom was an ability to understand beasts and birds. Their speech is not like our speech; they do not communicate in articulate "words" as we do, but more like feelings or intentions. They spoke of battle, of bloodlust, and a hunger for man's flesh. Among them rose a long, deep, resonant howl, seemingly from deep in the earth itself. My blood ran cold; it was the voice of their master: Crom Cruach, the lord of wolves.

While the warriors rushed into the chaos, Patrick, Afagdu and I lifted up our voices in a hymn. In the dim torchlight, Uther, tall and broad-shouldered, charged into the fray, lopping off a wolf's head as it was about to pounce upon him. Another he pierced through its muscular neck. There was wolf blood everywhere. Rushing to the aid of a townsman and his wife as the wolves encircled them, Uther slew all the beasts in a fluid dance of destruction.

Meanwhile, the wolves closed in about us, snarling, saliva dripping from their toothy mouths. Cold sweat formed on my brow as I looked into those flaming yellow eyes. Patrick struck the nearest wolf with his crozier, knocking it senseless.

"Back! Begone!" said the bishop to the other wolves.

Suddenly two wolves fell dead, penetrated by a single spear from the powerful arm of King Oengus. The king of Mhumhain charged in, slashing a wolf with his Hibernian short sword. Another wolf crouched behind him, ready to attack, but the hound Odarnat sank her fearsome teeth into his throat before he could attempt such an assault. The king, coming to the aid of his faithful dog, stabbed the infernal beast with his short sword, ending its life. In a flurry of death, Oengus and Odarnat struck against their hoary foes, biting, slashing stabbing, snarling. They acted as a single unit of annihilation, but still the wolves closed in, concentrating their numbers about the high king.

Then with a mighty shout, Uther rushed in, smiting the nearest wolf with Caledbur. The beast's severed head lay bleeding on the ground. The other wolves backed away, snarling with hatred, lest they too feel the bite of Caledbur.

"Thank you," said Oengus, reluctantly.

Uther looked at me, unsure what the king said.

"He said thank you," I translated.

A moment later came the wild, triumphant howl of Crom, calling his followers away to his gruesome feast. The wolves vanished as if by magic. My heart sank; he had found his victim.

We bore the wounded back into the great hall to be healed. Patrick, in addition to being a man of great faith, was a gifted healer and was much help in aiding the wounded. Fionnlagh, being a bard, knew much of herb-craft and, though blind, knew many healing plants by scent alone.

King Oengus came limping into the hall and sank into his chair with a thud. Immediately, Fionnlagh and I set about treating his wound.

"They took another," he said ominously. "Another mother deprived of her child. Damn him!"

"What is he saying?" asked Uther.

I repeated what King Oengus had said in Cumbric. His square jaw worked back and forth with rage. Uther hated to see lives needlessly taken.

"The more innocent blood he takes, the stronger he grows," remarked Afagdu. "At night, they come, terrorize the townsfolk, take their prey and then they vanish into the forest like smoke in the wind."

"We've tried hunting them down," said Oengus, "but they are too many. The only way to defeat them is to slay their master."

"Caledbur would kill him," I remarked.

"It's not that simple," said Afagdu. "Crom Cruach has bound his essence within the Crom Stone."

"What is the Crom Stone?" I inquired.

"A great black stone that fell from the sky," replied Afagdu. "Only Crom and his druids know where it is hidden."

"That isn't strictly true," said Fionnlagh. "I found it once."

"What? When?" exclaimed Oengus, "Why did you not reveal this before?"

"I was under a geas," explained the bard.

In those times, it was customary in Hibernia to make certain vows, called geasa, which could never be broken, such as abstaining from certain foods, or avoiding certain activities. At times they were imposed by a bard, or a king; other times they were self-imposed. One Gaelic king, for example, was forbidden from entering a house after three red-headed men, else he would suffer dishonor or death.

"Crom struck me with blindness so that I would not lead anyone else to the stone," continued Fionnlagh. "But I could only reveal the truth in the presence of the greatest bard in all the world."

I flushed slightly. It was indeed flattering to be called the greatest bard of all.

"Do you think you could find it again?" I inquired.

"With a bit of help, I believe I can."

"Praise the Lord!" said Patrick.

"Well, ain't that just a four-leafed clover!" exclaimed Conall. "What are we waitin' for?"

"Will someone explain what the devil is going on?" exclaimed Uther in exasperation.

I briefly related to him all that we had discussed, to which Uther replied: "Shall we leave at first light?"

Upon hearing what Uther had said in his own tongue, King Oengus grimaced.

"And who are you to be giving orders?" he snapped. "This is a Hibernian problem, and Hibernians should be the ones to solve it."

"There's no shame in asking for a bit of help, son," remarked Patrick. "Even our Blessed Lord did not do everything alone."

"Then we should put our trust in Him rather than these Britons," retorted Oengus.

Uther looked about him, confused once again.

"What are they saying?" he asked.

"Oh, some flumadiddle about Hibernians not needing any help from Britons," said Conall.

"All this aside," said Fionnlagh, "there is only one thing on earth that can destroy the Crom Stone, and that is the sword Caledbur, and there are but few men on this earth worthy to wield it. One of them is here, and you can either accept his help, or throw up your hands and whine about it!"

My eyes widened with wonder at Fionnlagh's frankness. I gathered later that bards in Hibernia were a highly respected, protected class. They were allowed to speak their minds in ways that others were not.

"Well..." grumbled Oengus. "I'll allow it. But if there be any sign of betrayal, I'll cut his throat from ear to ear!"

"What did he say?" inquired Uther.

"He says we'll do it," said Domhnall. By necessity, he was a natural diplomat and an expert at smoothing over tensions.

"We shall have a wolf hunt at first light," said Oengus. "In the meantime, we shall try to get a bit of rest for our eyes."

We bedded down for the night. The accommodations were comfortable enough, though I wished I had Creirwy by my side. My dreams were troubled with visions of battle: British men fighting Saxon invaders. At the time I had thought them merely to be dreams of the battles I had witnessed in times past, but later, it became clear that these were none other than visions of the future. Needless to say, I had an ill night's sleep.

4

Morning rose foggy over Hibernia; I had the impression that nearly all mornings were foggy there. After a hasty breakfast, we prepared for our journey into the wilderness. Oengus had many fine horses, which he graciously lent to the Britons for the quest. The king himself rode on a great white horse, perhaps the finest I had ever seen. I found out later that the Hibernians believed that only a king could ride on a white horse.

All of us mounted up for the journey into the green wilds, with the exception of Fionnlagh.

"Will you not be riding, Fionnlagh?" asked Oengus.

"No, my king," replied the bard. "I must feel the terrain, since I cannot see it."

"Quite sensible," replied Afagdu. "I will accompany you on foot."

"That's awfully kind of you, Afagdu."

"It is my pleasure," he replied.

With our final farewells, we then rode out of Corcach, following Fionnlagh and Afagdu as they hobbled into the dark forest. Peasants lined the streets, some to cheer their brave king and his war band; others to weep for us, certain that our mission was doomed to failure.

"I suppose I shall have to learn Hibernian if I am to survive this journey," stated Uther.

Patrick laughed. "It is not so different from Cumbric, my lord. If you like, I will teach you some common phrases."

"That would be of great benefit," replied Uther.

Throughout the day, as we journeyed through the rolling green hills Bishop Patrick and I educated Uther in the essentials of Hibernian grammar. The warlord at first found it challenging, but with time, he began to comprehend it. By nightfall, he was having a rudimentary conversation with King Oengus about hunting boar.

The forests of Hibernia were then much thicker than nowadays. Deer and wild swine roamed among the innumerable firs and oak trees, along with myriad other beasts, from the mundane to the fantastic.

As the sun went to his nightly repose, we made camp by a bubbling stream in the midst of the wood. Afagdu and I went off to fetch firewood in the gathering darkness of the Hibernian wilderness. The wood was silent, unnaturally silent. Not even an owl hooted in the trees. There was a certain oppressive heaviness to that sepulchral silence, as though all of nature had held her breath. Crom was on the move.

"We should return to camp," I whispered.

Somewhere in that stifling black stillness, a twig snapped. We bolted for the camp, running as fast as our legs would allow through the nighted wilderness until we reached the glen where we had built our camp.

"Taliesin, what is the matter?" asked Uther.

"Something in the wood!" I panted.

"Something large and terrible!" added Afagdu.

The men had no time to react before there was a great cracking of tree branches accompanied by the bone-chilling hunting cry of an ogre. The massive, ugly beasts crashed into the glen, swinging their tree-trunk clubs left and right. Instantly, the men drew their arms to defend themselves from the murderous band.

Spears and arrows studded the thick hide of the beasts like hedgehog quills, having little effect on them.

After gutting the nearest creature with Caledbur, Uther whirled about just in time to pull Oengus out of the way before he was crushed by a massive club.

"Thank you – look out!" cried the king, tossing his spear into the throat of an oncoming ogre, killing it instantly.

"Aim for the throat!" cried Uther over the noise of battle.

I did what little I could to defend my companions, tossing spears and javelins at the throats of the ogres, but there are limits even to my abilities.

"Taliesin!" cried Uther. "Take Fionnlagh and flee!"

Without another word, I took hold of Fionnlagh's hand and dragged her away from the battle. Into the gathering night we ran, heedless of where we were headed. This proved to be our undoing.

After glancing back to see if we were being pursued, I heard a sudden shriek from Fionnlagh. The ground seemed to vanish beneath my feet as down I fell into a black abyss. After that, all was senseless nothingness.

...

At last, Uther sheathed his sword. The ogres had retreated into the night, leaving carnage in their wake.

"Well, that was invigorating," said Conall.

"A very apt phrase, Conall," said Uther. "You have made a good accounting of yourself, it would seem. Is everyone well?"

"I appear to be in good shape, milord, thank you," replied the fisherman.

"Excellent."

"You fought well, Lord Uther," remarked King Oengus.

"Thank you, good king," replied Uther. "You were quite skillful as well."

"Thank you. Now, where are the bards at? Fionnlagh! Taliesin! Come hither and show yourselves!"

But no answer came.

Oengus called all the louder for them, and sweat streamed down Uther's brow. How would they continue the quest without the bards to guide them?

"Where have they got to?" asked the Hibernian king.

"Fionnlagh!" cried Afagdu frantically.

"I told them to flee the battle," replied Uther.

"What?" barked Oengus.

"It was too dangerous for them to stay. I could not have the bards be injured; the stakes are too great."

Oengus flew into a rage, striking Uther in the face. Uther braced as the king pulled back for another strike.

"Oengus!" shouted Patrick.

Domhnall and Conall caught hold of the enraged king, restraining him from beating Uther within an inch of his life. Wiping the blood from his chin, Uther glared at King Oengus

"You fool!" roared Oengus. "You might've sent them to their deaths! Do you even know what might be lurking in that wood?"

"I did what I thought best under the circumstances, your majesty!" protested Uther. "They were in at least as much danger here in camp as out there in the wild."

Oengus' nostrils flared like an angry bull as he glared back at Uther.

"I suppose you're right," said the king of Mhumhain at length. "Nothing to be done now but find them."

King Oengus let out a low whistle, summoning his faithful hound Odarnat to his side.

"Bring me something that Taliesin or Fionnlagh wore," commanded the king.

Afagdu produced a linen gown from Fionnlagh's pack. Odarnat sniffed the garment, taking her scent into her keen nostrils. Then Odarnat bolted into the wood following the trail into the dark forest.

"Come on, men! Follow Odarnat!" commanded the king.

Mounting upon his great white steed, Oengus followed the hound into the wood, his men following shortly behind bearing torches to lighten the darkness ahead. There was nothing else to do; either they must find the missing bards, or return to Corcach defeated.

5

I awoke with my head pounding like a drum. I groaned with pain as I attempted to lift myself from the hard ground beneath. Where was I? What had happened? My memory of what had just occurred returned to me in bits and pieces. I looked about, but there was little to see as little light filtered down from the surface into the deep cavern we had fallen into. I could barely make out the shape of Fionnlagh sitting beside me.

"Are you alright?" she asked.

"My head!" I groaned.

"Here, chew this," she said, placing something into my hand. I did as I was told. It was fibrous and bitter; I surmised that it was likely willow bark, a well-known pain reliever.

"Thank you, Fionnlagh," I said. "Where are we?"

"I am not certain."

I looked up the vertical shaft we had fallen down. There seemed to be no means of escape from that fissure.

"Well, we are not escaping the way we came in. I suppose we shall have to wait until Uther and Oengus come to rescue us."

"I'm not sure that would be wise, Taliesin," replied Fionnlagh. "There's something very peculiar about this cave."

"How do you mean?"

"The stones," she replied. "Something about them doesn't feel right."

Like most Hibernians, Fionnlagh went unshod and therefore had a better sense of the terrain than I did. There seemed to be a deep, rumbling, throbbing sound coming up from the earth beneath. The ground heaved gently upward, before slowly sinking down again. It was so slight that one less sensitive than Fionnlagh might not have noticed it at all. To my horror, I came to the realization that this was no ordinary cave. We had stumbled upon the lair of a conqueror wyrm.

Long before any man looked out upon a star-studded sky, the conqueror wyrms ruled the primordial chaos. The elves and gods slew most of them in a great and terrible war. Most lay dead, their bones having become a riddle to puzzle the latter generations of men. Others vanished into the black voids between the spheres. Some lay slumbering in the deep places of the earth. Evidently, we had stumbled upon one of these.

Cold sweat bedewed my brow.

"We need to leave this chamber – now!" I whispered.

Slowly and carefully we arose from the cave floor, creeping through that unholy nest of shadows toward what we hoped would be an escape. Fionnlagh, being accustomed to traveling without sight, led the way through the tomb-like chamber. Over the smooth scales of the massive dragon we went, treading cat-like upon the huge coils so as not to disturb its slumber.

At long last we seemed to come to the end of the huge beast, breathing sighs of relief.

"Where to now?" I inquired.

"I suppose," replied Fionnlagh, "we ought to find an alternate route back to the surface and hope Uther and King Oengus can find us."

"Agreed."

Taking my hand again, Fionnlagh led me through the subterranean corridors, her staff tapping rhythmically on the stone walls, feeling her way through the winding corridors of gloom.

...

Dawn came red over the forests and fens as Uther and his men followed Odarnat, hoping to find their lost companions.

"Anyone got any food?" asked Conall. "I feel like I'm going to die of starvation!"

"We don't stop until we've found Fionnlagh and Taliesin," responded Oengus.

"Oh, come on, Oengus! We've been walking all night, at least let us get a wee bite to stave off hunger."

"We cannot expect to find our companions with minds dulled by hunger and weariness," added Uther.

"Fine," grunted Oengus.

It was about that moment that Odarnat began to bark imperatively. The king steered his horse to the dog's side. The hound stood at the edge of a large fissure in the earth; just wide enough for a man to fit into it.

Uther and the others quickly joined the pair, staring down into the shadows below.

"Looks like a cave," remarked Conall.

"Is that right, Conall?" sneered Domhnall. "I thought it might be a tavern!"

"Hold your mouths!" ordered Oengus.

"Taliesin!" called Uther. "Are you down there, lad?"

"Fionnlagh!" cried Afagdu.

The only answer was his own echo. Still the dog sat by the cave, refusing to move an inch.

"If Odarnat believes Fionnlagh is in that cave," said King Oengus, "That's good enough for me. Anyone got a rope?"

One of the Hibernians produced a coil of strong rope, which Oengus then tied to a stout pine nearby.

"By your leave, majesty," said Afagdu, "I would like to enter the cave first."

Oengus stared at the novice for a few moments, before nodding and handing him the rope.

Into the bowels of the earth he went, feeling his way down the shaft. Once at the floor of the cave, Afagdu called our names with a loud voice. The only response was the yawning emptiness of the cavern.

"What have you found, Afagdu?" asked Uther.

"Nothing, sire," replied Afagdu. "If they ever were here, they've moved on."

Oengus looked at Patrick and frowned.

"Should we try to find them?" asked the king of Mhumhain.

"I think it would be wise to look," replied the bishop.

Oengus nodded. The king then divided the company into two groups; one to explore the cave, and the other to stay with the horses. Thus equipped, Oengus, Uther and the rest of their company joined Afagdu in the blackness below, unaware of the slumbering wyrm beneath them, who was, in turn, unaware of them.

...

Things continued in Camelot much as they had for the days and years before Uther had left for Hibernia. Diplomatic agreements were made, justice was carried out, farmers tended the land and craftsmen plied their trades in the markets.

One fine afternoon, Creirwy, consumed with boredom, decided to spend the day in the marketplace playing a small flute. There she sat amongst the tradesmen going about whatever it was they were doing, playing a merry tune on the little instrument. She had decided to compose a lullaby for the royal babe who was to be born, and simply needed to put the right notes together. She later told me that she had dearly wished I had been there to lend a hand; while she was a talented musician, she admitted that I was the better composer. She wondered to herself what may become of me in Hibernia, facing Crom Cruach without her by my side.

Her attention wandered away from these thoughts when a raven landed on the cobblestones nearby. As she watched the bird, it transformed into the shape of Menuu the magician.

Creirwy had not seen the sorcerer in days. Where had he been? What had he been up to? Like myself, Creirwy never really trusted Menuu. There was something unsavory in his aspect that we did not care for, nor could we put a proper name to whatever it was until long after the events of this tale.

"Menuu," greeted Creirwy. The magician looked upon her with something resembling contempt in his murky green eyes.

"Good morning, Creirwy," he said, as though it was a dirty word.

"Where have you been?" asked Creirwy.

"My comings and goings are not your concern," replied Menuu, curtly. "Why? Has anyone needed my expertise?"

"I doubt if anyone truly needs your expertise, magician," replied Creirwy in an equally curt tone.

The magician's features contorted into a scowl. He walked away at a fast pace, as if he had a purpose in mind. Being vaguely curious about Menuu's sudden reappearance, Creirwy followed him at a distance, attempting - though poorly - to look as though she was not following him at all.

Menuu bowed as he entered the court of King Emrys.

"Menuu," said Emrys. "Good of you to happen by. Where have you been?"

"Here and there," replied the magician. "I have just returned from Londinium. Lord Vortimer reports that the Saxons are gathering strength again."

Emrys' countenance darkened.

"They have joined forces with the Picts and are riding westward," continued Menuu. "They are probably heading this way. Lord Vortimer has gathered his war-band and is on his way here; he shall be here tomorrow."

Emrys stroked his square jaw.

"The Saxons would be foolish to try a direct assault on Camelot," said Gorlois.

"Perhaps," said Emrys. "But without Uther and Caledbur--"

"Emrys, you are a mighty war-leader," exhorted Nimue. "You do not need Uther or the sword to defend your kingdom."

"Let those filthy savages come!" exclaimed Creirwy suddenly emerging from hiding. "We can take them."

A broad smile made its way across the king's features.

"Very well," he said. "We shall prepare for battle. Menuu, fly out again and make an estimate of their numbers."

"By your command, my liege," said Menuu, bowing. The magician then transformed into a raven once again and flew away.

6

"Watch your step, Conall!" said Domhnall.

"You watch yours, ya big ox!" retorted Conall. "You stepped on me foot thrice now!"

"Quiet, both of you!" scolded Oengus. "We do not know what is buried down here!"

They entered a larger chamber. Massive columns stretched upward into the gloom above. Sculptures and frescoes lay all about, depicting ancient kings, gods and beasts of all descriptions in hideous splendor. Bones of misshapen creatures lay on the stone-tiled floor of the chamber; some bore the semblance of men, others were clearly of a more bestial nature. Through a small opening in the roof above came a shaft of light to illuminate the chamber.

The men paused, looking about them in wonder and befuddlement at the cyclopean ruins of a kingdom lost to time. Uther had the feeling that he had just uncovered something far older than anything he had ever encountered.

"Where the devil are we?" asked Conall to no one in particular.

"Part of ancient Hyperborea," answered Afagdu. "This is an evil place. We should leave, quickly."

"We are not alone," said Oengus.

The entire company went dead silent, listening for the slightest sound. The king's keen ears detected something shuffling and scratching somewhere deeper in the cave. Slowly, he drew his short sword.

Screaming out of the ancient ruins came an army of small, ugly creatures. They bore the semblance of man, but were less than half of a man's height and were hideous to look upon.

"Boggards!" cried King Oengus.

The diminutive inhabitants of the ruined city screeched in their loathsome tongue – though one could scarcely call their language intelligible – firing crude arrows, spears, and sling stones at the invaders. Others flooded in bearing clubs, maces, hammers, axes and other crude implements of war, bludgeoning their opponents.

Domhnall cursed. Conall raised his voice in a wolfish howl, charging toward the horde of villainous creatures, thrusting his spear into the wicked mass of monsters. Left and right, Uther swung the mighty sword Caledbur, shearing them down like a reaper cuts down sheaves of grain. Uther laid low all who dared approach, the famed sword dripping with black blood.

Bravely did the warriors fight against the innumerable mass of miniature monsters in that cyclopean city. Suddenly, the boggards let out a terrible shriek. In a flooding mass, they ran to the shadows. The warriors stood in the great chamber, surrounded by small ugly corpses.

"Well, that was easy," said Conall, wiping the perspiration from his brow.

Out of the yawning blackness came a great bellow as of an ox.

"Damn it, Conall!" said Domhnall. "Why'd you have to open your gob?"

Into the chamber charged the massive, bestial forms of the ogres. This was their abode and they would defend it.

"Scatter!" cried King Oengus. The men did as they were told, running off in all directions to confuse their foul enemies. As they did back at the camp, they aimed their weapons at the throat, where the beasts were most vulnerable.

With a great shout, Uther raced toward the monsters. Swinging Caledbur low, he smote one in the leg, cutting it down at the knee. Uther lopped of his odious head as he fell. Another ogre came at Uther, swinging a crude mace over its ugly, ape-like head to slay Uther, but a javelin found its mark in the creature's neck. Uther looked to see what hand had thrown it; there stood King Oengus, grinning from ear to ear. Both turned abruptly as the unexpected sound of Afagdu's voice came to them from across the cavern, shouting out a command in the unholy tongue of Annwyn. It echoed through the ruined city, which had once been home to such a language. The ogres cried out in terror, retreating into the eternal night of the Hibernian underworld.

"Why didn't you think to do that before, lad?" asked Domhnall.

"I did not think it would actually work," replied Afagdu.

"No matter," said Oengus. "It worked, and that's all that counts. Come then, let's find our companions."

"I hate to be a wet blanket, your majesty," said Conall. "But it seems you've been shot."

The king looked down and beheld a dart embedded in his leg.

"Oh damn it!" he exclaimed. "There's likely to be wyrm poison in that dart, if I know the boggards."

After removing the dart, they dressed the wound the best that they could. Uther's brow furrowed; it seemed things had gone from bad to worse. Without medicine from Taliesin and Fionnlagh, Oengus would surely perish in that stygian abyss. Still, Uther wore a brave face as they pressed on, keeping these thoughts to himself.

...

The clouds hung low over Camelot that morning as the king left the morning liturgy, descending the steps with his queen on his arm. Gorlois and his family came down the steps behind the king, Creirwy coming last in line as they stepped out into the cool morning air.

The morning's restful atmosphere was suddenly interrupted by a tumultuous noise erupting from the gates of the city, as of many voices crying out.

Rushing to the gate, Emrys found many ragged peasants flooding into the city, many with serious injuries. Accompanying them were a band of warriors who bore the emblem of Londinium.

"What has happened?" asked the king.

"We have come from Caerwent, your majesty," said one karl. "The Saxons have invaded. The village is destroyed!"

Anger burned in Emrys' heart. His fists curled into tight knots.

"King Emrys!" hailed a familiar voice.

"Vortimer!" said Emrys, gladly.

Vortimer dismounted his steed, embracing his dear friend the high king, saying, "It is good to see you again, your majesty."

"As it is to see you, Vortimer," said Emrys. "Would that your coming to Camelot were under more favorable circumstances."

"That is the way of things, majesty," remarked Vortimer.

"Ah, Queen Nimue!" he hailed as the queen approached with Gorlois and Igerna, Creirwy trailing behind them.

"Hail, Lord Vortimer!" said Queen Nimue.

"All is well, I trust?"

"If all were very well, you would not be here," replied Emrys.

"That is true."

"Troubled times make for great deeds," said Gorlois.

"Creirwy, will you see that the wounded are taken care of?" asked Emrys.

"Of course, your majesty," replied Creirwy with a curtsey.

The lady then went off to do the king's bidding, fetching the apothecary and securing lodging.

"If they would only plan these invasions better," remarked Igerna. "We could have prepared a welcoming party for them."

Emrys laughed heartily. "And so we shall!"

"Aye, I imagine the king has a welcoming gift for them," quipped Vortimer. "I do not see Uther about. Is he well?"

"He is off fighting in Hibernia," explained Emrys.

"With Caledbur, I might add," said Nimue. "Which is why we need your help more than ever."

"I understand," said Vortimer.

"We shall prepare a war band and ride out today, if possible," said Emrys.

"Allow me to refresh my men and my horses and we shall be ready to ride by midday."

"Excellent," said the king.

...

Meanwhile, deeper and deeper into the caves Fionnlagh and I went, hoping against hope that there would be some opening somewhere further down the next passage. The only sound was the constant tapping of Fionnlagh's stick and my own breathing.

"Wait a minute," whispered Fionnlagh. "Do you hear that?"

I strained my ears, trying to discern what it was she was hearing. Indeed, there was a strange rhythmic sound echoing through the cave. It sounded almost like music. We followed the sound to wherever it might lead. As we came close and the sound grew louder, it was evident that it was in fact music - merry music of pipes and flutes, drums and lyres playing somewhere in that gloom.

Soon there came a cool, blue-green light up ahead as we drew nearer the sound of merriment. The light emanated from the luminous mushrooms which grew in Hibernia's underworld. In the light of these, I perceived that we were not in a cave at all, but some sort of hall. The walls were not of natural rock, but were carven with intricate designs.

As we passed through that ancient hall, a warm light became evident further down the passage.

"I will go first," I said to Fionnlagh.

As I crept close to the source of the illumination, the music grew louder. Finally I found an opening into a spacious chamber, wherein were many little folk dancing and singing to the sound of the instruments.

7

King Oengus grew weaker and weaker. Eventually, he was forced to lean on Domhnall for support as the poison worked its way through his blood. The torches began to fail; soon they would have no light at all, and be left in the charnel deeps. Many wondered if this cave would be their tomb.

"Let's stop and rest a minute, then," said Conall.

"Nay, Conall," said Oengus, weakly. "We have to press on to find the bards."

"Your majesty," said Domhnall, "with all due respect, we ain't found 'em yet, and you're not getting any stronger by looking."

"We can spare but a moment to rest," said Uther.

"Did I ask your opinion, Briton?" snapped Oengus. "We press on! Find the bards so I may be healed and we can complete the quest."

"My lord, we are lost!" Uther responded with strained patience. "We do not know where the bards are, or even if they still live. We should at least take a moment to think about what we are to do next."

"You want me to die down here, don't you?" snarled Oengus.

"Nay, good king," replied Uther. "I want you to live out your days and defeat Crom."

"Liar!" croaked Oengus. "You only want the throne of Mhumhain for yourself!"

The king drew a dirk, lunging at Uther with whatever strength he had left. Uther quickly stepped out of the way, dodging the blow.

"Your majesty, stop this!" cried Domhnall. "You're speeding the poison along!"

"That's what this British dog wants!"

Oengus lunged again. Conall, while being a loyal friend of the king, knew that this was madness brought on by the poison, and therefore took action. The fisherman rushed in, taking hold of Oengus, restraining him from stabbing Uther.

"Unhand me, Conall!" growled Oengus.

"It's for your own good, majesty," replied Conall. "Can't have you stabbing the only man who might be able to kill Crom!"

The strong fisherman wrestled the king to the ground. Oengus was weakened by the poison, but still full of the vigor Hibernian men are known for.

"Your majesty," said Uther, "with all due respect, if I wanted you dead, you would be by now. I could have let those ogres kill you back at the camp."

"I suppose you're right," Oengus grunted in response.

There was suddenly a sound of slow clapping echoing from nearby in the chamber.

"Excellent performance, gentlemen," said a voice.

Into the torchlight came a short, manlike being, clapping his diminutive hands.

Uther reached for his sword. "Who... or what are you?"

"Rollo Goodfellow at your service," said the creature, bowing low. "I am a hobgoblin. Welcome to my realm."

"What is it you want, then?" asked Conall.

"Oh, peace, happiness, contentment, gold. But I suppose you're wondering what I'm doing here. My hunting party has been following you since you killed all those ogres. Excellent job, by the way. I am wondering why _you_ are here. Man's realm is above. This is our abode."

"We are searching for our companions," said Uther. "Two bards, a young man and woman. Would you happen to have seen them?"

"You're the only big folk I've seen down here."

Uther sighed deeply.

"Would you be able to do something for our king?" asked Domhnall. "He's been shot with a poison arrow."

The hobgoblin examined the prone king, looking closely at the festering arrow wound.

"I know of a cure for this poison," said Rollo, "but it is not easy to obtain. It will cost you."

"What's the cost?" groaned the dying king.

"One of you must swear an oath to me, that you will do a favor for me. Anything I ask. I may call upon you at any moment, whether it be tomorrow, in a fortnight, or many years from now."

"I'll do it," said Uther.

"Bad idea," cautioned Afagdu. "The little folk of the underground are treacherous. You do not know what they may ask you to do."

"I have no choice, Afagdu," replied Uther. "I must save the king."

"Do you solemnly swear to do whatever I require?" asked Rollo.

"I do solemnly swear," said Uther.

Rollo grinned. "Excellent! Now, let's go back to my chambers where he may be treated."

The war band gently bore up the King of Mhumhain, carrying him down the passage, following Rollo Goodfellow and his hunting party.

"Why would you do that, Uther?" asked Oengus.

"Because someone had to."

"You don't know what they'll ask you to do!"

"You're right," said Uther. "I can only trust that it will be a light burden, whatever it is."

...

I had heard tales of the small folk of the underground called hobgoblins. They are a race resembling man, but much smaller, with blueish skin, and large, sharp eyes and ears for living in darkness. They can be capricious toward those who offend them, but loyal to them that do them honor.

I stood at the edge of the chamber, uncertain what to do.

"The Sidhe!" exclaimed Fionnlagh. The maid pushed me aside and marched fearlessly into the chamber. There was a great commotion amongst the little folks as she drew near, many of them greeting her with a glad cry. I followed cautiously after her, approaching them with great care.

"Friends," said Fionnlagh, "this is Taliesin, Prince of Bards."

The hobgoblins bowed respectfully before me; the profession of bard is much lauded by the Hobgoblins.

"We are honored by your presence, Taliesin," said the foremost among them. "Please, come and sit down! Rest from your travels."

I gladly took the small chair they offered me; a rest for my tired feet was indeed welcome.

"Bring mead for Fionnlagh and the Prince of Bards!" ordered the hobgoblin. The serving women were quick to respond, bringing me a cup of mead and a dish of porridge in quick order. I looked at the refreshments, unsure of what to do. I had heard tales that those who taste of the food of the underworld are unable to ever leave.

"It's alright, Taliesin," said Fionnlagh before taking a draught. "It's quite safe."

I shrugged, taking a small sip of the mead offered to me. It was fine mead indeed; perhaps the best I had ever drunk. I took a bit of the porridge, which was also quite good.

"How do you know these people?" I inquired.

"I did them a good turn some time ago, and they helped me when I was first blinded," replied Fionnlagh. "I have been kind to them ever since."

"I see," I replied.

"Many in Hibernia mistrust them."

"And they are right to do so!" said one of the hobgoblins with a hearty laugh. "We're as cutthroat as the craftiest pirate, and cunning as a fox!"

"With the exception of Delgo here, of course," added Fionnlagh.

The hobgoblin laughed.

"Say, where is Rollo these days?" inquired Fionnlagh.

"Oh he's off hunting the ogres," said a female hobgoblin. "Said they were more active than usual. He'll likely return in a day or two."

"We ran afoul of them ourselves, Elenora. Well, be sure and tell him I missed him."

"You're not staying for a day?" asked Elenora.

"Nay, we have a quest we need to get back to."

"And what would that be?" asked the hobgoblin named Delgo.

"Killing Crom Cruach," I replied.

The hobgoblin laughed. My face twisted into a scowl; it irked me that he seemed so dismissive of our errand.

"You can't kill Crom. No one can."

"We believe otherwise," I retorted.

"Then you're either very brave or very foolish."

"Perhaps a bit of both," I replied.

The hobgoblin let out another hearty laugh and downed a draught of mead.

"If you would simply show us the way out of this cave so that we may continue the quest, we would be grateful."

"Surely," replied Delgo. "But only if you grace us with a song, Prince of Bards."

The hobgoblins rarely do anything without some sort of payment and while I wished to return to the surface world, I understood that they would not help us without some sort of exchange. I therefore took my lyre upon my lap and began to play a song of one of the great battles Prince Gwyn fought against Lord Arawn of Annwyn. The little folk were enchanted. Some clapped, some cheered, some wept. It was indeed a grand time for them.

"Prince of Bards indeed," said Delgo. "I'll guide you to the surface, but I would beg that you play but one more song for us. Consider it a boon."

I pondered his request for a few moments; I did wish to find King Oengus and our war band, but I also knew that having the hobgoblins on our side might be an asset in the coming battle against the wolf god.

As I opened my mouth to sing, there was a sudden noise from the other end of the chamber, as of many horns blowing. I looked up to see a company of hobgoblins enter the chamber bearing spears and poleaxes. Behind them were none other than Uther and his band.

"Lord Uther!" I shouted with joy. My heart dropped however, as I saw Domhnall and Conall bearing the frail King Oengus.

"Rollo, what is all *this*?" shouted Elenora, angrily.

"Some guests for dinner," replied the chief hobgoblin. "Now, go fetch the potion to wyrm poison, quickly! This poor fool hasn't much time left!"

Elenora did as she was told, gathering up her ragged skirts and running to another chamber as fast as her feet would carry her.

"Fionnlagh!" cried Afagdu, moving quickly toward the maid. The two embraced, glad to be reunited.

"I feared you had been lost," said Afagdu.

"Have you so little faith in me, Afagdu?

The son of Tegid chuckled.

I raced to King Oengus' side as they laid him gently down.

"What happened?" I inquired.

"He was shot with a poison arrow," replied Uther.

"Uther," croaked Oengus. "You're a better man that I thought you were."

"Save your strength, good king," replied Uther.

"Nay," replied Oengus. "I do not have much left; I ought to spend it well. Take care of my kingdom."

"But your majesty -"

"Do not let the gods get the upper hand again!"

Just then, Elenora returned with a round jug. She slowly poured the contents down the king's throat. The king coughed slightly and then went silent. We feared it was too late. Taking up my lyre again, I sang a healing song, hoping that it might speed the potion along.

Suddenly Oengus coughed and gasped, sitting bolt upright.

"What the devil did you just give me?" he wheezed. "I feel like me chest is a-boil!"

"He's fine!" said Conall, patting the king of Mhumhain on the back.

"Fine? Famished, more like! Bring meat!"

To this day, I know not what the hobgoblins put in that magical brew that caused such a change over Oengus, but I have never seen anything quite like it since. Helping their king off the floor, the Hibernians sat Oengus at a low table where the hobgoblins brought him some stew.

"I'm a wee bit peckish meself," said Conall. "Ye wouldn't happen to have any more of that stew, would ye?"

"If you're going to drop in unannounced and demand to be fed, you'll be expected to work for it," said the diminutive woman. "Follow me."

Shrugging their shoulders they followed the lady.

"You too, handsome!" commanded Elenora.

Uther furrowed his brow.

"Yes, you! Come along, then! There's work to be done."

Uther joined the company in another chamber, which appeared to be a sort of kitchen. She gestured to a barrel of roots, saying: "Make yourselves useful; peel and cut those roots for supper."

The warlord sighed, and set about the task of peeling and cutting the vegetables, as did the fishermen. Domhnall and Conall seemed to be the masters of the craft, cutting and peeling roots twice as quickly as Lord Uther. The brothers laughed and joked, turning the task into a contest to see which of them could peel the most roots. Uther, meanwhile, worked in sullen silence.

"Is there something the matter, sire?" asked Conall.

"I do not understand it; we are warriors, not scullery maids."

Domhnall chuckled. "We all have to do what is right in front of us, milord. Whether that is riding into battle or peeling carrots. We don't always get to choose what is handed to us."

Uther nodded sullenly. He knew the Hibernian was right, but it still galled him to be doing common servant's work, as he saw it.

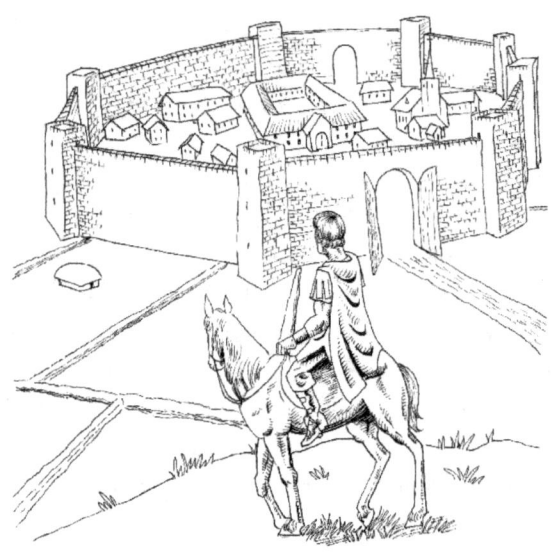

8

The cavern filled with the savory scent of hearty stew as we took our seats at the low table the hobgoblins had set for us. Lord Uther told us of all that had occurred since our hasty retreat from the battle with the ogres. I listened attentively, remembering every word he spoke for the annals.

Once we had eaten our fill, King Oengus arose from the table and said: "Well, it's time we head off."

"Ah, but you've only just arrived," said Rollo Goodfellow. "Will you not stay a night and rest?"

"Nay, Master Goodfellow. Patrick will be waiting for us on the surface."

"I see. Well, at least allow me to guide you back safely."

"We would be grateful if you did so."

We all arose and followed the hobgoblin through the wretched corridors of darkness beneath Hibernia. Most of us had to stoop under the low ceilings, but I could feel the fresh air from somewhere ahead.

"What have you been up to these past few years, Fionnlagh?" asked Rollo.

"I've been in the employ of King Oengus," replied the maid.

"Ah, good for you! I knew you'd make good one day. Off to pay Crom back for what he did to you, eh?"

"I suppose," replied Fionnlagh.

"You suppose?"

"In a way, I think Crom almost did me a favor."

"What?" said Rollo in astonishment.

"Since I've come to rely more on other senses, these have grown stronger; my hearing has grown keener, for example, and this has made me a better bard."

"Well, marvels never cease!"

After a time of walking through the dark corridors of the caves, I finally saw above me a blanket of starlight. It was night; we had been in those dank caverns for an entire day, and I did not even know it.

"Here you are, then," said Rollo. "Welcome back to the surface. I wish you good luck in your quest. Give Crom an extra stab for me."

"Thank you for your hospitality, sir," said Uther. "We shall not forget it."

"Think kindly of me when you ascend the throne," said Rollo.

"What do you mean by that?" queried Uther.

"I've a feeling Camelot will be requiring your presence very soon, your lordship."

"Wherefore?" asked Uther.

"Toodle-pip!" said the hobgoblin as he ran back down the cave.

"Get back here you... hedge-pig!" shouted Uther, but the hobgoblin either did not hear him, or simply chose not to. Likely the latter, as Uther's voice was quite loud.

Uther bristled. "Well, I suppose he is not going to give us any answers now. Come, let us see if we can find Patrick."

...

King Emrys buckled his sword belt about his waist. He wished that Caledbur was by his side again, but such was not the case. He was a competent warrior with or without the elven blade, but he still desired to feel its weight in his right hand. It reminded him of his father.

Nimue entered the room, placing her hands on his strong shoulders.

"Are the men ready?" he inquired.

"So far as I can tell, my love," replied the queen.

"I am ready as well."

"You are wanting of one thing."

The queen drew near and pressed her warm lips into Emrys.

"For luck."

"Would that I could take you with me," sighed Emrys.

"Keep me in your heart, and I shall be."

Nimue placed a helmet upon the king's head.

"The Lord keep you safe."

Emrys marched out into the courtyard where his men and the men of Londinium were assembled, ready to embark on a holy quest to rid the land of the heathen. Mounting his mighty white steed, Emrys rode out at the head of the company, as peasants threw flowers on the path before them.

Out they rode into the wild country beyond Camelot. The king suddenly paused, turning his horse about to gaze upon the fair city he loved. He had a peculiar look in his eye, as though he was leaving, never to return. Turning away, he spurred his horse onward as his men sang a song of battle; perhaps it was the last time he would join them in the chorus.

...

Our feet ached as we walked through the Hibernian night toward our camp - or at least we hoped that's where we were headed. Our torches had long burnt out, so we were forced to rely solely on Fionnlagh's leading to get us back to where we should be.

The pitch-black forest grew unnaturally silent.

"Wait a moment," said Fionnlagh. "We are not alone."

Out of the darkness came a chorus of long howls. Crom had found us.

"Run!" said Uther.

We beat a swift path through the darkened wilderness as the wolfish feet chased after us. A warrior cried out as a wolf tore into his flesh, dragging him off the path. Uther drew his sword, the blade glowing like the light of a full moon. He struck at the beast like a blacksmith striking red hot steel. More wolves closed in about us. Steel glinted faintly in the starlight as the men drew their weapons. We would be fighting blind, but we had no choice in the matter. We were in Crom's element; this was his domain.

Domhnall and Conall howled like mad dogs as they hacked with their weapons in a crazed fury. Uther and King Oengus fought back to back, their swords hacking their demoniac foes to pieces. Even Fionnlagh fought; her staff whistled through the air and landed with a dull thud on canine skulls.

Without further delay, I put my fingers to my lyre strings and sang with all my might. The forest lit up as millions of fireflies gathered about us. At last we could see our enemies!

Then came the baying of Odarnat as the great hound charged into the glen, accompanied by the booming voice of Patrick. With them came the rest of the company who had been left with the horses and provisions, crying out with battle-mad fury.

"Odarnat!" cried King Oengus gladly.

Using his crozier as a weapon, Patrick struck the vicious beasts mercilessly. There was no fear in his eyes, nor was there any hesitation in dealing out savage blows to the opposition.

Together, we beat the hounds of Crom back into the stygian night. Uther sighed with relief; he had had quite enough excitement for one day.

"Thank you, Reverend Father," said the warlord.

"You are most welcome, my son," replied Patrick.

King Oengus knelt down, vigorously stroking the thick brown hair of Odarnat as the dog repeatedly licked the king.

"Ah Odarnat! I feared I'd never see your face again."

"What happened down there?" asked Patrick.

"It's a long story," said Fionnlagh.

"I will have to tell you on the way back to camp," I added.

"Indeed!" said Patrick. "I would like to hear it!"

Together, we made our way back to camp, as I told the tale of our exploits in the Hibernian underworld, recounting with enthusiasm our encounters with the hobgoblins, with Uther and Oengus' account of the battle with the ogres. The bishop listened with great interest until our arrival at the camp. We then bedded down for a well-earned rest before the final leg of the journey the next morning.

-9-

The cookfires blazed in the British camp that night as the warriors sat about them, exchanging stories and jokes. There seemed an atmosphere of merriment about the whole camp; no one feared the Saxons, it seemed.

King Emrys sat silently staring into the flames as they danced and sparked before him. There seemed to be a melancholy in his eyes as he ate his stew.

"What's the matter, my lord?" asked Lord Vortimer. "You've barely touched your stew."

The king looked up at Vortimer as though the proconsul had simply appeared out of nowhere.

"I am well, Vortimer. Simply contemplating the battle."

"I see."

"We shall prevail, good king," said Gorlois. "Though their numbers are great, the Saxons have never been able to break us, not even when bolstered by Tegid and Ceridwen."

"This is true."

Out of the corner of his eye, Lord Vortimer saw something glint like mail in the firelight, just out of sight. He dismissed this as a trick of the light and nothing more, continuing to converse with Gorlois and Emrys about times past when they had faced Saxons together in battle. Again, something moved in the shadows. It was small; perhaps a curious field mouse or some other harmless beast of the field.

Suddenly, Vortimer saw again the glint of mail directly between King Emrys' feet. Vortimer began to speak a warning to the king, but it was too late – the adder had already bitten Emrys in the lower part of the leg. The king cried out. All the men leaped up at once. Gorlois attempted to capture the reptile, but it had slithered away into the dark.

"What happened?" asked one of the warriors.

"King Emrys has been bitten by a viper!" replied Vortimer.

Gorlois stripped the king's breeches away from the adder bite. It was already beginning to bruise.

"It's a deep bite, your majesty.

Emrys groaned. "I knew this day would come, but O God! Why now?"

"Do not worry, good king, we shall take you back to Camelot, and Creirwy and the queen may yet heal you."

"Nay, Vortimer," said King Emrys grunting with pain as the venom coursed through his veins. "My time has come."

Vortimer's eyes welled up with tears. "No! I will not allow it!"

"It is not in your power to prevent."

"Do not just stand there gaping!" said Gorlois. "Bring a wagon; we shall carry him to Camelot!"

"It is of no use, Gorlois," moaned Emrys. "I am about to die."

The men ignored his words, loading Emrys onto a wagon strewn with skins and cloaks to make the journey more comfortable.

Loading the king into the vehicle, Gorlois urged the horses forward at a quick pace, while Vortimer rode in the wagon with the king.

"Vortimer," said Emrys in a voice barely above a whisper.

"Yes, my liege," replied Vortimer.

"Make certain that my wife and child are cared for. And tell them that I loved them until the very end."

"You will tell them yourself," said Vortimer.

"I fear that I shall not."

Through the night they raced back to the city, the light of the moon as their only guide. Finally in the still hours before dawn they returned to the gates of Camelot. The men clamored about as Father Dubric approached, Sylvia the apothecary by his side.

"Emrys!" cried Nimue, racing to the wagon.

"What happened to him?" asked Creirwy who had come with her.

"Adder bite," said Vortimer.

"How long?" asked Sylvia.

"Just after sunset," replied Gorlois.

"I have never seen an adder bite work so quickly," said Sylvia.

"His heartbeat is weak," said Nimue, concern in her eyes.

Wasting no time, Dubric began to pray fervently that the king be healed of his infirmity.

Sylvia examined the wound in the light of her oil lamp; the skin around the bite was black as night.

"There is devilry in this!" she exclaimed.

Emrys turned his head toward his weeping queen, his gray eyes nearly swollen shut, and smiled.

Together, Nimue and Creirwy joined in a healing song, but it was of no use; the high king's strong heart gave out. Emrys Wledig breathed his last just as the sun arose. Vortimer and Nimue lifted up their voices in lamentation. Great was the grief of Camelot.

...

A thick fog enshrouded us as we rode through the gray Hibernian wood toward our goal, the blind bard leading us on, aided by Afagdu. A fetid stench of rot permeated the fog, and I perceived that we had come to the edge of a bog.

"Wait, now," said Domhnall. "Oughtn't we to think about this a wee moment? One must be concerned about knuckers, after all."

The fisherman was correct. Throughout the countryside in those days, there lived large, lizard-like creatures known as bog knuckers. Their venomous bite made them a danger to any and all who dared approach a bog. I had had my own run-in with the knuckers some time before this, but that is another story.

"This way," said Fionnlagh as she led us southward around the border of the bog. "There's a safer way along here. We are close to the stone."

Her staff tapping the earth before her, the poet led us onward toward what we hoped was a safe path to the Crom Stone.

Suddenly, the earth gave way under her feet and with a stifled cry, she fell into a deep, muddy pit. No one would have seen it had she not fallen in.

"Fionnlagh!" cried Afagdu as he took hold of her arm. With all his strength, Afagdu attempted to heft Fionnlagh from the muck, but something seemed to be holding her down. A great knucker thrust its hideous, scaly head above the water, its long, lithe body strangling Fionnlagh. With a single blow from his short sword, Afagdu cleaved the reptile's head from its body.

"Are you alright, Fionnlagh?" he asked once he had freed her from the hole.

"A wee bit shaken, but I'll be fine in a moment," she replied.

Over the bog, through the ancient trees came once again the call of Crom Cruach, summoning his forces to battle in the dreadful speech of the wolf.

"Damn!" exclaimed Oengus.

Squirming and slithering came the knuckers, like worms from the infernal depths, blocking our path. Drawing our weapons, we prepared to fight the reptilian adversaries as best we could.

"Come on, men!" said King Oengus. "Let's send them back to Hell where they belong!"

"Taliesin!" called Afagdu. "Clear the way before us and I shall defend Fionnlagh from behind."

I nodded, reaching for my short sword. However, I thought better of it; there are times to draw the sword and there are times for less violent means of combat. Sheathing the blade, I instead took my lyre from my back and began to play. The knuckers hissed, parting before us as we proceeded through the bog toward our ultimate goal. Patrick, seeing our progress, rode out before us clearing the way of knuckers with his crozier. They feared the very sight of him.

Out of the wood came the gray shapes of the wolves, snarling, ready for the kill. Spears and arrows flew at the wild beasts mad with bloodlust. Odarnat, ever loyal and brave, ran before her master into the fray, fending off the canine horde before the high king of Hibernia. Domhnall and Conall fought side by side with spear and short sword, Conall laughing like a mad man. I had not seen such a wild frenzy since the day Lord Arawn attacked Camelot.

Uther's horse fell to the ground with a thud, a knucker coiled about its legs. Three wolves charged in for the kill, but Uther slew the three of them in one fluid stroke. Rising from the mire, he ran the knucker through the head with Caledbur. The ferocious weight of a wolf struck Uther's back, taking him to the ground, but a spear from the hand of Oengus ended its ferocity.

"Are you well, Uther?" asked Oengus, offering his hand to the warlord.

"I shall be," replied Uther as he arose.

"We'll handle these hellions," continued Oengus, "you follow Fionnlagh to the stone! Finish the quest! Save Hibernia."

Uther nodded. "I shall not fail!"

Uther joined our little company as we marched toward the Crom Stone, Caledbur flashing like a shooting star in his hand as he slaughtered our savage foes.

Into a dark grove of blackthorn trees studded with many large boulders we plodded on. Fionnlagh led us through a narrow crevice in the walls of rock, when from above us came a low snarl. I looked up in terror as a great black shape pounced upon Uther, taking him to the ground. It was Crom Cruach himself, his great teeth gleaming white as he attempted to sink them into Uther's throat.

Uther wrestled on the leaf-littered ground with the beast, his sword having fallen from his hand. Drawing our short swords from their scabbards, Afagdu and I attacked, stabbing and slashing at the black wolf, but this only seemed to anger him. The beast turned on us, his great jaws snapping. I leaped back, narrowly avoiding his fearsome bite.

"Go back to your father, the Devil!" cried Patrick as he struck the beast with his crozier.

Crom snarled and snapped at the bishop.

"You do not frighten me, holy boy!" growled the wolf god.

"Nor do you frighten me!"

"Unhand him, you demon!" commanded Fionnlagh.

Crom growled savagely at the girl bard.

"What does it take to teach you a lesson, girl?" he said in a low, rumbling voice that seemed to come from the earth itself. Crom lurched slowly toward Fionnlagh, licking his chops. Afagdu leaped upon the wolf god with a mighty shout, sinking his blade into the wolf-god's foul flesh. Crom barked, turning on the son of Tegid with lightning speed. Taking him by the tunic, he threw Afagdu against the rocky wall of the crevice.

In desperation, Uther reached for Caledbur, but the blade lay just beyond his grasp. Suddenly, the blade leaped into his hand, as if by its own accord. Taking advantage of the moment, Uther thrust Caledbur straight through Crom's black heart. The warrior shoved the limp body of the beast off of his muscular frame and got to his feet. Puffing and panting from his efforts, Uther stared at the corpse, believing the battle to be done.

"Now," said Uther, turning to Fionnlagh, "about that stone."

"This way," the girl replied.

A hellish laughter rumbled from the immobile wolf. The body seemed to lose all form, melting into a shapeless heap upon the earth. It coalesced before our eyes into the vague form of man, clothed in black, a long sword appearing in his hand as he arose from the ground. He stood a head and shoulders taller than Uther.

"You cannot defeat me, Pendragon!" roared Crom.

Uther cursed; Crom Cruach still lived!

Crom then let out a great and terrible howl, beckoning his forces. Wolves flooded in, snarling, biting, snapping, barking.

"Christ be my strength!" yelled Patrick, drawing his sword from the sheath.

Together, Afagdu and Patrick set about the work of killing the wolfish foes.

Taking my lyre from my back, I sang with all my might, summoning any and all birds and beasts of the wood to our aid. Down from the sky came a flock of birds, while badgers, foxes and even squirrels and mice flooded in from the fields and glens, attacking the hellish beasts.

Crom Cruach swung his sword, narrowly missing Uther. Uther countered the attack, but Crom parried his strike. The Pendragon backed away from the black god's attacks, blocking and slashing as Crom drew nearer. Uther, stumbling over a rotting log, fell on his back. Crom moved in for the kill, but Patrick tripped him up with his crozier. Uther rolled to safety.

Crom Cruach turned on the bishop, drawing his sword back to strike him, but Afagdu, with a beast-like roar, leaped onto the back of Crom, stabbing him in the neck. Casting Afagdu to the earth, the Lord of Wolves raised his mighty blade and ran him through the torso.

"Afagdu, no!" I cried in dismay, running to render aid.

"What's happened?" asked Fionnlagh.

"He is sorely wounded," I replied, "I will care for him; you need to help Uther!"

Fionnlagh nodded.

Crom raised his sword again to strike Patrick, but Uther quickly charged in, slicing off the black god's sword hand. Crom roared, kicking Uther in the chest. The warlord staggered back from the blow.

"Uther! Reverend Father! Come quickly!" cried Fionnlagh from a rocky ledge. Uther and Patrick did as they were bade, scrambling to follow the bard. Atop the outcrop was a great mound, a tall standing stone, black as pitch and smooth as marble. This was what they had been seeking. Uther ran toward the accursed monument, but Crom, seeming to appear out of nowhere, stood in his way; a new hand had grown where the old had been severed. The black god attacked with a slashing blow, striking Uther's arm. The mail shirt took the brunt of the blow, however.

Uther stuck back with Caledbur, wounding Crom in the thigh. The black god only laughed.

"Crom!" cried Patrick.

Crom turned. Patrick stood right next to the stone, eyes ablaze with righteous fury as he pushed it to the ground with his crozier. Crom howled with rage. Uther stabbed the black god through the back.

After pulling his sword from Crom's torso, the Pendragon ran to the mound, raised Caledbur high and thrust the blade into the black stone. With a sound like thunder and a brilliant flash, the Crom stone shattered. Crom Cruach bellowed one last time before melting into an inky black puddle of pure malice.

Meanwhile, the fighting ceased as the wolves let out a great howl and fell to the ground. A change came over them; they turned from wolves into men, lying naked upon the fen.

Afagdu lay on the ground, Fionnlagh beside him, holding his misshapen hand as tears streamed down her face.

"I suppose it had to end this way, Gwion," he said to me. "Here on the battlefield."

"You're going to be alright, Afagdu," I replied, taking some herbs from my purse.

"How, Gwion?" he asked. "In case you had not noticed, I have had a blade in my chest."

I placed the herbs upon his wound, and taking Fionnlagh's hands, I pressed them to the leaves.

"Fionnlagh, press down on these herbs."

"Afagdu!!" cried Patrick as he strode into the glen.

"Reverend Father," groaned Afagdu. "Tell me you defeated him."

"The power of Crom is broken," said the bishop.

Afagdu smiled grimly. "Then it was not all in vain."

"Bishop Patrick, come place your hands on him and pray."

I took my lyre from my back and sang a healing song. Gradually, the life returned to Afagdu's face. My song ended, Fionnlagh carefully removed the herbs from the wound.

"You are healed!" she exclaimed.

"Thanks be to God!" said Patrick, crossing himself.

The bard and the bishop helped Afagdu to his feet again. Fionnlagh hugged him tightly, kissing him on both cheeks.

Leaning him on our shoulders, Fionnlagh and I brought Afagdu down from the outcrop to the bog, Patrick and Uther following us.

Domhnall and Conall approached at a swift pace.

"Oi! Patrick!" shouted Conall. "I take it our work here is done?"

"Aye," replied the Bishop.

A cheer erupted from the warriors, combined with a cry of anguish from the former werewolves.

"Repent of your folly!" cried Patrick. "Your god lies dead. You may see his resting place for yourselves."

Upon seeing Uther and Patrick, Crom Cruach's servants cowered and fled into the forest. The Hibernians began to chase after them, but King Oengus stayed them with his hand.

"Leave them run," said the king. "They'll come back to fight another day."

One, however, remained; a young maid of auburn hair sat upon the bog, naked but for a spiked leather harness. Oengus furrowed his brow at her.

"And who might you be, young lass?" he asked.

"I am the one you've called Odarnat these past few years," replied the maid.

Oengus' eyes widened. "Odarnat? My *hound* Odarnat?"

"Aye," she replied with a smile. "Crom Cruach turned me into a hound some time ago before you found me. My name is Eithne, daughter of Cremthainn."

Oengus helped the maiden off the ground, blushing somewhat and placing his tartan cloak about her.

"What's the matter, your majesty?" asked Eithne.

"Well, it's... just that you were a hound not long ago. We hunted game together. I stroked your fur. I gave you food from my table."

"You need not be ashamed, your majesty," replied Eithne. "You cared for me, and for that I am grateful."

"You risked your life for me," said Oengus.

"And I would do it again many times over," replied the maid. "You are a good man, King Oengus."

Oengus blushed again as Eithne gently kissed his cheek.

"What's the matter? It isn't as though I've never kissed you before," said Eithne with a wink.

Oengus laughed. "I suppose I shouldn't count on your company on my next hunting trip."

"I wouldn't say that," replied Eithne. "I always enjoyed our hunting trips."

Oengus smiled. "Perhaps we'll have many more hunting trips, then."

"I'd like that very much."

Placing Eithne on a red horse, King Oengus led her and his men out of the bog and back toward Corcach, singing a song of victory as we went.

-10-

    King Emrys' mortal remains lay in the church that eventide, awaiting the funeral ceremony and entombment. Queen Nimue lay quite still on the floor next to the body of her king, having exhausted herself with weeping. Creirwy, too, remained in the sanctuary, refusing to leave her queen's side. Vortimer sat on the floor, leaning against a wall, his blue eyes staring straight ahead.

    "I should have said something," moaned Vortimer. It was the first word he had said all that day.

    "What do you mean?" asked Creirwy.

    "I saw the serpent before it struck Emrys; I should have warned him."

Creirwy frowned. "Why didn't you?"

"I thought it was a trick of the firelight."

"It could have happened to anyone, Vortimer."

Vortimer sighed. "But why was I so unlucky that it happened to me?"

"There's no use crying over spilt milk!" chided Creirwy. "Now you can either sit there wallowing in self-pity, or you can get up and do something about it. We have a kingdom to save."

Vortimer took a deep breath. "Yes, the kingdom. You're absolutely right."

Vortimer then arose, leaving the church at a swift pace, Creirwy following closely behind.

"What are you doing?" asked the proconsul.

"Coming with you," replied Creirwy.

"You cannot; you're a woman."

"Try and stop me."

Vortimer paused, furrowing his brows at the lady.

"Creirwy, this is an incredibly dangerous undertaking."

"You think I do not know this?" retorted Creirwy, crossing her arms. "I have faced the howling horde of Arawn in battle."

"One man is already dead, and battle has not even begun!"

"Which is exactly why you should bring me along," said Creirwy with a smirk.

Vortigern sighed. "I cannot dissuade you, can I?"

"My husband already tried."

"Fine then; get to the armory and at least put on something sturdier than that gown."

Creirwy smiled, heading straightaway to the armory. As they marched along the streets, a raven flew down from the heavens and landed not far away. Menuu had returned.

"Menuu!" exclaimed Creirwy.

"Where the devil has he been?" asked Vortimer.

"Oh, who knows."

The pair approached the magician.

"Menuu, do you know what's happened?" inquired Creirwy.

"To what are you referring?" asked Menuu.

"The king is dead."

A look of shock contorted Menuu's face. Perhaps a bit *too* contorted; as though he were attempting to falsify surprise at the king's murder.

"What are we to do now?" he asked. "Uther is gone and has taken Caledbur with him. The barbarians are coming with three-score thousands of their number. Even with the men of Londinium, there is not enough!"

"Well, then do not stand there mewling, you pusillanimous pea-fowl!" barked Creirwy. "Turn into your raven-shape, fly to Dyfed, Ceredigion and anywhere else we have allies and get reinforcements!"

The magician gave her a dour expression; he was not accustomed to being ordered about in such a manner, especially by a woman.

"You heard the lady!" commanded Vortimer.

"By your command, your grace," replied the magician, before returning to his raven shape and flying away.

"Come on, then, Creirwy," said Vortimer. "Let us get you outfitted."

Creirwy nodded as they continued to the armory.

...

Dubric was loath to wake the queen; her grief was great, and she needed her rest. However, the people needed to know that their leaders had not abandoned them. Thus he leaned down and gently jostled the slumbering Nimue. The queen looked up at the priest through drowsy eyes, still red from weeping.

"My queen, you must awake. You have had neither food nor drink all day, and it is nearly evening; think of the child."

"The child," groaned Nimue as tears slid down her fair cheeks.

"You must be strong for the child and for the people, milady. They must know that their leaders have not abandoned them."

"I know, Father," she moaned, "but how can I be strong?"

"Trust in the Almighty. He is wiser than we. Your strength comes from him."

Nimue sighed. The thought of leading the kingdom and raising a child without her husband by her side was more than she could bear. Still, she must be strong; without strong leadership in Camelot, the kingdom would surely fall before the Saxon hordes, leading to centuries of darkness.

Dubric helped Nimue off the floor. The queen straightened her gown and wiped the tears from her eyes. Leaving the church, the two of them started back to the great house, the citizens in the streets clearing the path for her, sorrowful expressions on all their faces. Emrys was a well-beloved king, and everyone felt the loss.

Out of the stables came Vortimer, Gorlois and Creirwy, riding on great war horses, outfitted for battle.

"My queen," said Vortimer. "We ride to meet the Saxons."

"Creirwy?" said Nimue quizzically. "Where do you think you are going dressed like that?"

"I am accompanying the men," said Creirwy. "They may need my expertise."

"She insisted upon it," said Vortimer. "I had the distinct impression that had I not agreed, she would follow us unawares; this way, at least we can keep an eye on her."

"Be *very* careful, my dear sister," said Nimue.

"Naturally," replied Creirwy.

"Make no more delay! Godspeed!"

"Thank you, your majesty."

The warriors and the lady rode out through the great timber gates, heading eastward to join the men on the front with all haste.

Nimue, meanwhile, paused as she arrived in the outer courtyard of the great house of the King. Turning to the gathering crowd she took a deep breath and made the following oration:

"People of Camelot... Britons, valiant men and women from the noblest knight to the humblest peasant. You know by now that your king is dead. But this is not the end of Camelot. We shall, by the grace of the Almighty, endure the trial into which we have been thrust. The brave men of Britain are riding out now to put a stop to the Saxon invaders, and with your prayers and support, they shall be victorious."

A murmur of approval spread through the crowd.

"Long live the queen!" cried Dubric. All the citizens echoed the rallying cry. Nimue then gave orders to have provisions brought within the city gates, on the chance that Vortimer and his men might be unsuccessful in repelling the Saxon hordes.

...

Afagdu walked arm in arm with Fionnlagh just ahead of me on the road to Corcach.

"Why so silent, Afagdu?" asked Fionnlagh.

"I have much to think about," he replied. "I nearly died today, you know."

"I understand," replied the bard.

"I am rethinking my vocation," he continued, unbidden.

"Oh?"

"Yes. I am beginning to wonder if it would be right to become a monk."

"What makes you say that? You'd make a fine monk."

"I am not certain I would. You see, there is someone – a young woman – to whom I feel my heart is drawn."

"Oh," said Fionnlagh, her voice falling. "Tell me more about this young woman."

"She is the loveliest woman I have ever seen," continued Afagdu. "She is fair of skin and fair-haired. She is ever most kind and gentle, and she sings like a bird."

"She does sound wonderful," said Fionnlagh.

"She is. I thought it impossible that she might enjoy the company of one so grotesque as I, but they say love is blind."

A moment of silence passed between them.

"Fionnlagh, that young woman is you."

Fionnlagh drew in her breath.

"I have felt the same for some time, Afagdu," she said at last. "I didn't wish to tell you, as I feared it would deter you in fulfilling your calling."

"I suppose I should speak to the Bishop," said Afagdu.

Fionnlagh wrapped her arms about Afagdu's neck and kissed him on his misshapen lips.

I smiled; Afagdu had found his peace. The one who once tried to slay me had found love at last. It was a beautiful thing to see.

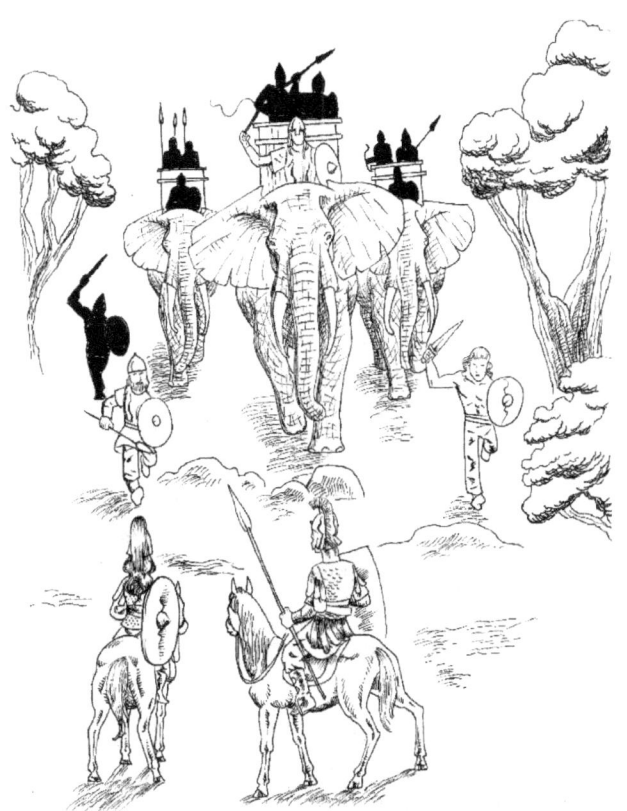

It was dark when Vortimer, Gorlois and Crierwy arrived at the camp where Emrys had been bitten. The men stood at attention, concern for their king written all over their faces.

Vortimer drew in his breath, his sorrow darkening his countenance. "The king is dead."

Many men gasped with shock; some fell to bitter tears immediately; others crossed themselves.

"We cannot mourn him as yet," continued Vortimer. "There is work to be done. The Saxons care not about our grief. They are coming to bring destruction upon us, whether we are ready or not. Our task is to stop them. For the king and for Camelot."

"For Camelot!" the men echoed.

...

My heart beat through my chest as I sat up in my cot. I looked about. Day was just breaking over Hibernia, and Uther would awaken soon. I needed to tell him what I had seen. Stepping over to Uther's bed, I shook him violently awake. Instantly, I felt the cold steel of a dagger at my throat; Uther always slept with one under his pillow.

"Fear not, my lord," I said. "It is I, Taliesin."

The Pendragon withdrew the dagger.

"Taliesin?" he growled. "What's the meaning of this?"

"We must return to Camelot immediately!"

"Whatever for?"

"I have had a dream. A terrible dream. The kingdom is in grave danger."

Rising from the bed, Uther put on his clothes, making no further delay.

"Everyone, wake up!" he said in a loud voice. "We must make ready to return to Camelot! Taliesin has had a dream. Something terrible is happening."

With that, the men immediately got dressed and began to pack for the departure. I ignored the groans and the speculation.

Bishop Patrick stood upon the shore with King Oengus by his side, Eithne's slender hand wrapped about the king's muscular arm. To his left stood Afagdu and Fionnlagh, holding hands.

"The grace of the Holy Trinity go before you, Lord Uther," said Patrick, blessing Uther.

"Amen, Reverend Father," replied Uther.

Oengus' great arms enveloped Uther in a tight embrace.

"I am sorry I ever doubted you," said the high king of Hibernia.

"All is forgiven, your majesty," replied Uther.

"Well, Domhnall and I better be heading back to Argyll," said Conall. "The wife is probably wondering what's become of us. So I suppose this is farewell, until we meet again."

"Farewell, Domhnall and Conall McCallum," I said. "Until we meet again."

"Taliesin," said Afagdu. "I never properly thanked you for sparing my life."

I smiled. "Think nothing of it, brother."

"Ah, but I am no monk."

"I did not mean it in that way."

Afagdu smiled crookedly.

"I suppose I should thank you as well," said Fionnlagh, "for saving this man's life."

"If you ever need me, I will be here," said Afagdu.

"And I shall be in Camelot."

"Farewell, Gwion, Prince of Bards."

With that, we set off for familiar shores.

...

The forest lay shrouded in mist as the gallant men of Britain rode toward their adversaries. Creirwy could practically feel their malice radiating toward them through the silent trees.

Gorlois paused.

"What is it?" asked Creirwy.

"We are not alone," replied the lord of Kernow. "I know how the Saxons fight. This is a perfect place for an ambush."

An ear-piercing shriek echoed through the forest as Saxon and Pictish warriors flooded the glen, their eyes wide with bloodlust. They were not armed with mortal weapons; no, theirs were of the type made and used in Annwyn and Bala – mighty swords and axes and those terrible ballistae which shoot lightning and fire.

Drawing their weapons, the fighting men of Britain charged fearlessly into the barbarian horde. The clash of steel reverberated throughout the glen. Blood, both Saxon and Briton, watered the earth beneath their feet. It was madness; but Creirwy had seen worse sights. On the left hand and the right fought Vortimer and Gorlois, defending her from any and all who dared come close. Gorlois emptied his quiver into the ever-tightening circle of barbarian foes, while Vortimer washed his spear in their blood.

"At least let me do something!" cried Creirwy in dismay.

Just then a Pict attacked Gorlois from behind, but Creirwy impaled him through the torso.

"Good job," said Gorlois.

Then came such a noise as Creirwy had not heard in a very long time; like loud trumpets of the damned, calling over the wilderness. Into the glen charged beasts never seen among the Saxons before. Great and terrible they were - twice the height of a man, even a Saxon. They were covered in thick, wrinkled hide, like a coat of impenetrable mail. Two great white tusks protruded from their jaws like javelins, and between those tusks was a great, long snout, dangling down like a fifth limb from its bulbous head. They were elephants. On their backs were great litters, from which spearmen and archers shot their deadly hailstones upon the Britons.

Vortimer's eyes widened with horror at the sight. There was nothing left to be done; there was no way they could defeat such a foe. "Retreat!" he cried, but the savage warriors closed in about them, cutting off their escape. The proconsul fought to the best of his ability, despite the close quarters. By his side stood Gorlois, fighting like a madman.

Crying out in the elvish tongue, Creirwy summoned the trees to their aid. Roots and branches bent and curved, forming a wall about the glen and holding off the elephants and their barbaric riders. It was temporary, but it might buy them time. Weeds and vines stretched up from the earth, tangling about the legs of the Saxons and their horses.

"Ha! That will teach them!" shouted Creirwy in triumph. "Come, Vortimer!"

Looking at her protector, Creirwy's heart sank. Vortimer's face contorted with pain. He looked down at the Saxon spear-head thrust through his chest. Coughing blood, he fell from his horse.

"Vortimer, no!" cried Creirwy, leaping from her steed.

Kneeling down next to the proconsul, she held his head in her hands.

"Run, Creirwy," gasped Vortimer. "Run while you can! Save the kingdom."

Creirwy cried out in a loud voice.

"Come, Creirwy!" cried Gorlois. "We must go!"

"We cannot leave him!" replied Creirwy.

"We will not!"

Leaping from his steed, Gorlois lifted the dying man onto his own horse, while he and Creirwy rode upon the other.

The horde overran the glen. Away rode Gorlois and Creirwy as fast as they could, Crierwy's loud cries echoing through the wood. Thorns and briars spring up behind them at Creirwy's bidding, closing off the way. The sorrows of Britain increased.

...

Queen Nimue lay in troubled dreams that early morning. She spent much of the night weeping for her husband, longing for his comforting embrace, praying that Vortimer and the fighting men of Britain would be successful.

"Queen Nimue," said a slight voice.

The queen opened her eyes to gaze into those of Morgana.

"What is it, child?" asked the queen.

"The men are returning from the battle," replied the young maid.

Immediately, Nimue arose from the bed and, dressing hastily, she went out to meet them. Lady Igerna, the wife of Gorlois, patiently awaited the queen in the outer courtyard, her brows furrowed. Evidently, she had feared for her own husband's safety as well.

"Forgive the rude awakening, my queen," she said.

"There was nothing rude about it, Lady Igerna," replied the queen, gently stroking Morgana's black hair. "Let us meet our returning champions."

Through the gates rode the dejected men of Britain, Lord Gorlois at their head. His face, normally somber, seemed even more melancholic than usual.

"Lord Gorlois, what has happened?" asked the queen.

"The Saxons were better prepared than we thought," replied the lord of Kernow. "They came upon us unawares. The slaughter was... too great."

"And where is Lord Vortimer?" asked Nimue.

"He fell," replied Gorlois, holding back tears.

Nimue nearly collapsed, and would have, had not Lady Igerna been there to hold her up. The sorrow was too great to bear, and she wept inconsolably. The lord and lady of Kernow bore the weeping queen back to the great house where she might rest and regain her strength.

Meanwhile, Creirwy's heart beat furiously within her chest, pounding with grief and anger. How could this happen? How could a group of rabble challenge the might of Camelot? How dare they bring a princess of Avalon to her knees? In that moment, she decided that she would make it her personal mission to ensure that they would be punished for their arrogance.

Returning to the armory, she removed the mail and other accouterments of war, and marched immediately to our room at the great house. There, she put on one of my older tunics and a pair of my breeches. Then, taking a cloak, a bag and a staff, she made her way to the gates of Camelot.

"Where are you going, Creirwy?" squeaked a little voice from behind her. Morgana, overcome with curiosity, had evidently followed Creirwy to discover her purpose.

"I am going to obtain help," replied Creirwy. "I need you to stay here. You must not breathe a word of this to anyone. Do you promise?"

Morgana nodded, smiling broadly.

"Good. I hope to return by tomorrow morning. Take care."

With that, Creirwy, in the guise of a man, left Camelot and departed into the wilderness.

-12-

The crickets sang their twilight song as the earliest rays of the dawn glowed on the Eastern horizon. The time was right. *Where was Gwyn?* Nimue wondered as she paced back and forth on the terrace of the great house. She had sent for him hours beforehand. He had plenty of time to get there from Avalon, unless he was out on a mission.

Finally there came the silver wings of a white owl, landing silently on the wall before transforming into the shape of Gwyn. The elf-prince removed his war-mask, something he only did in the presence of close friends and relatives. His scarred face was stricken with grief.

"Dear sister," he said, embracing Nimue. The queen wept bitterly in her brother's arms, her silver tears flowing onto his tunic. Prince Gwyn held her tight, stroking her soft dark hair, his own tears mixing with hers.

"I am sorry I did not come sooner," said the prince. "I was delayed by Lord Arawn's forces."

Nimue wiped the tears from her face and looked up into her brother's emerald eyes. "There is deeper grief than the loss of Emrys in your eyes."

"It is Father," replied the prince, his voice husky.

Nimue's heart sank.

"What has happened?"

"He has fallen ill; I fear it may soon be time for him to rest with his fathers."

Nimue fell to weeping again. Not only had she been deprived of a husband and a close friend, but soon she would be without a father. Regaining her composure at length, she said: "There will be time for mourning later. Now the kingdom is in peril."

Gwyn sighed. "Of course there is more. The death of the high king could not be enough grief."

"Uther has departed for Hibernia with Caledbur and the Saxons have joined forces with the Picts. They are riding toward Camelot as we speak, aided by Tegid and Ceridwen's black arts, no doubt."

"I would offer aid if I could," said Gwyn, "but Arawn has sensed that Father is growing weak, and has sent his forces to attack our outer defenses. I simply cannot spare even one man. We are sorely beset upon."

"But if Camelot falls--"

Gwyn laid his strong hands on Nimue's shoulders.

"Camelot shall not fall. You shall stand. The Almighty shall keep you from falling. He has gifted you with great powers; use them."

Nimue nodded, her lips quivering.

"I must return to the front; my men need me. May the Almighty go with you and guide you," said Gwyn.

"And you as well, my brother."

The elf prince returned to his owl shape and flew away into the burgeoning dawn. Nimue, overcome with grief, went to the church, where she knelt down before the lifeless body of her husband and wept bitterly.

...

Creirwy followed no trail or map but only her instincts as she beat her way through the silent wood. In time she came upon the opening of a cave. Staring into the black abyss before her, she was almost afraid to enter. Fear was not an emotion Creirwy was accustomed to; in truth, she feared very little, contrasting with myself.

"Hold on, then," said an unfamiliar voice. Creirwy spun about. A red bearded dwarf sat on a large boulder, his ax in his hand.

"Beg pardon, Mr. Dwarf," said Creirwy with a curtsey. "I am looking to enter the cave."

"For what purpose?" asked the dwarf.

"I need to speak to the dwarf lord who dwells within. It is a matter of the utmost urgency."

"What is your name? Who is your father?"

"I am Creirwy, daughter of Tegid the Bald."

The dwarf guard went pale and gripped his ax a bit tighter.

"Tegid's folk are not welcome in these lands."

"I am come on behalf of Camelot," replied Creirwy, placing her hands on her hips.

"I was not aware King Emrys was in the habit of keeping such company."

"My loyalty is to the house of Emrys. Tegid may go to Hell!"

"And how am I supposed to believe you? Get you hence, witch!"

"Oh a witch, am I?"

Creirwy took a step toward the creature, glaring threateningly into his beady, dwarfish eyes.

"If I were really a witch, you would be much more respectful. Now you will take me to see your lord, or I will turn you into a... a toad!"

The dwarf nodded shakily, leading the way into the caves. In time the sound of deep, resonant singing came to their ears, accompanied by the rhythm of smithing hammers and the scraping of blade on grindstone.

A fog of warm steam filled the smithy, smelling of dwarf-sweat and hot metal. Some of the dwarves paused their labor to stare at the lady as she walked through their midst.

The dwarf guard escorted her to a great dwarf with a thick white beard hanging almost to his knees. He was examining a particular crystalline object with a magnifying glass.

"Almost flawless," he said with delight.

"My lord," said the dwarfish guard, timidly. "This lady has come from the surface world to seek you."

The dwarf lord glared at Creirwy with suspicion.

"And who are you and what do you want?" he asked.

"I am Lady Creirwy of Camelot. I am a friend of your ally, Emrys Wledig."

"Emrys I know," said the dwarf lord. "Now why would he send you?"

"He did not, my lord," replied Creirwy. "The king is dead."

The dwarf went pale. "How did this happen?"

"Adder's poison," replied Creirwy.

The dwarf was silent for a span. "Have you merely come here to give me the news?"

"Nay, Lord," replied Creirwy. "I have come to ask your aid. The Saxons have mustered all their armies and they are marching toward Camelot as we speak."

"Camelot has withstood worse," grumbled the dwarf.

"Yes, but not without help."

"And what help would you ask me for, eh? The treaty I signed with Emrys only ended hostility between dwarf kind and mankind; it did not promise aid in time of distress."

"Listen here you short, fat, ugly, churlish ironmonger! I did not come down here to hear your stupid excuses! Our king is dead. Uther has run off to Hibernia with the sword Caledbur, and we are severely outnumbered!

"I did not even come down here to ask you to risk your men's lives! I came here to ask you to do what you do best: make weapons. Lots and lots of them. Bring them to Camelot and you will be paid handsomely."

There was another span of silence in the smithy. A hundred pairs of beady eyes stared at Creirwy with shock and wonder. A loud guffaw from the dwarf lord broke the spell. His short, muscular frame shuck with mirth.

"You're a young lady with some iron in your blood!" he exclaimed. "Are you certain you are not part dwarf?"

"So you will help?"

"Certainly!"

With a loud voice, the dwarf lord then shouted some orders to the smiths, who immediately returned to their hammering, building instruments of war for the men of Camelot.

-13-

All through morning prayers Nimue wrestled with her doubts and anger. She wore a brave face for the sake of the common folk, but in her spirit was a fire of passion. All she wanted to do was cry out "why?". *Why are all these evils come upon us?* She asked in her spirit. *Why has the Almighty turned his face from us?*

It was then that Father Dubric read the words from the Psalm:

> Come, behold the works of the LORD, what
> desolations he hath made in the earth.

He maketh wars to cease unto the end of the
earth; he breaketh the bow, and cutteth the spear
in sunder; he burneth the chariot in the fire.
Be still, and know that I am God: I will be exalted
among the heathen, I will be exalted in the earth.
The LORD of hosts is with us; the God of Jacob
is our refuge. Selah.

Then she understood. Evil would have its hour upon the earth, but it would not prevail. No sorcery, however powerful, could stand against the power of good. She left the sanctuary, filled with renewed hope and resolve for the coming battle

As she made her return to the great house, a strange sight met her gaze; in the town square was a dwarven cart, where several dwarves distributed weapons to the men of the city and even some of the women. Atop one of the carts stood Creirwy, handing forth mighty swords, battle axes, war-hammers, maces, ballistae, spears and other weapons of dwarfish make to the defenders of the city. There was an almost festive atmosphere about the place.

"What is all this?" inquired Nimue.

"Our armaments," replied Creirwy with a mischievous grin.

"The lady prevailed upon us to lend aid with our craft," said a dwarf.

Nimue laughed in astonishment. "Surely there shall be no end of marvels!"

"Alright men, gather 'round!" shouted Creirwy. "Come get your weapons!"

It was at that time that Menuu returned, flying down from the sky in his raven shape and landed among them in the shape of man.

"What news, Menuu?" asked Queen Nimue.

"The warriors of Dyfed are on their way, but I fear that the Saxons shall arrive first," replied the magician.

"And we shall be ready," replied Nimue.

Turning to the company of warriors she said in a loud voice: "Every man to the walls! The barbarians shall have far more than they bargained for once they reach the city!"

The men followed the instructions of their queen, climbing up to the walls of Camelot with their magical weapons

"I had best get to the armory," said Creirwy.

"You have risked yourself enough," said Gorlois. "Your husband would be wroth if he knew I was allowing you to charge into battle time and again."

"Besides," said Nimue, "Father Dubric and the apothecary will need you in the infirmary."

"Oh, alright," Creirwy huffed.

As they prepared for battle, Father Dubric said his final blessing over the men on the wall, preparing them for a day of warfare.

"Whatever happens, whatever you see, stand your ground and show no mercy!" said Gorlois in a loud voice.

And thus they waited for the coming of the savages to Camelot.

...

Evening came, and with it a cloud of gathering dust on the horizon, signaling the arrival of the combined barbarian forces. The men readied their weapons for the battle as the enemy approached the city gate.

"What the devil are those?" asked one of the men as the great beasts came into view.

"Elephants," replied Gorlois, "Have no fear. Fire when ready!"

Fire, spears and javelins rained down upon the barbarians as they came screaming to the gate of Camelot. The elephants charged in at the front of the company, slamming their great tusks into the mighty gates like living battering rams, heedless of the fray taking place about them.

All around, the screams of dying men and the fierce grunts of the elephants hung in the air. Attempting to ascend to the top of the walls, the Saxons threw grappling hooks onto their battlements, only to be repulsed by the defending Britons. Indeed, Gorlois had not seen such fierce fighting since his younger days when he and Emrys fought the forces of Vortigern.

Through all of this, the battering of the elephants came still thundering against the gates, heedless of the fight all about them.

Queen Nimue had ascended one of the high towers to view the battle. Upon seeing the utter chaos at the gate, she raced down the steps, running as quickly as her feet would carry her to the church, where Father Dubric had set up a hospital.

"Creirwy!" she cried as she entered. "I need you!"

Without another word, Creirwy left the church and ran through the street to the tower. The two ladies joined their voices in song, summoning a great storm. The wind howled, thunder crashed and the rain fell. But the elephants, driven mad with the fury of battle, continued to batter the gates. For all the dwarfish craft that had built those gates, they would not last much longer.

"Prepare for a breach!" ordered Gorlois.

Immediately, the men took up their weapons and ran to the gate.

"Whatever comes through that gate, stand your ground!" said Gorlois.

Standing ready, the men watched in quiet resolve as the gates cracked and splintered before the might of the elephants. The archers and slingers loosed their projectiles, aiming of the eyes of the elephants, blinding the first two that came in, while battle-mad swordsmen charged toward them, hamstringing the beasts.

...

I thought it odd how the storm had swept up so quickly as we rowed up the Severn Estuary to Camelot. A sickening feeling came over me as we neared the harbor. The sounds of battle could be heard over the howling winds. The oarsmen quickened their pace. The moment we were near enough to the docks, Uther drew the sword Caledbur and leaped from the ship, I and the other men following swiftly after.

About the same time came the clarion call of the horn of Dyfed; King Kynyr had arrived. Together we charged toward the fray. The Saxons were not expecting an attack from the rear and were ill-prepared for the battle-mad fury of Kynyr, nor were they ready for the onslaught of Uther with his conquering sword, Caledbur. The sight of the elephants attacking the gates had in no way deterred Uther. He charged toward the nearest of the beasts and thrust Caledbur deep into its guts.

The great animal gave a low groan as it bled out, staggering back and forth until it finally fell. The Saxons who had been riding it sprang into action, drawing their swords and knives to attack Uther, but the Pendragon laid many of them low with Caledbur. He had killed an elephant; what made them think they were any match for him?

With a massive crack, the gate of Camelot finally broke. The elephants charged in. There was little the men of Camelot could do against them, even with their dwarfish weapons.

"Kynyr!" I cried. "Help me!"

The lord of Dyfed nodded, lowering his spear. The Red King cleared the way before me, impaling any and all opposition in my path as I raced to the front of the battle.

Then out of the fog of war rode a mighty Saxon man on a black horse. His golden beard was spun with silver threads and a savage look emanated from his ocean-blue eyes. A wolf pelt was upon his back and a great spear was in his hand. It was Horsa, brother of Hengist. Emrys had slain Hengist in his youth, and it seemed Horsa had come to settle the score.

Uther marched steadily toward the king of the Saxons. Horsa charged in, spear trained on Uther. Uther knocked the spear aside with Caledbur. He then thrust the sword into the earth. Horsa came back for a second attempt, but Uther dodged the spear point, taking hold of the shaft with both hands. Horsa, unprepared for the raw strength of Uther's mighty arms, fell from his steed, still grasping the spear.

The Saxon king stood up just in time to dodge a swipe from Caledbur and draw his own sword. The two men, both masters of sword-craft, both forged in the field of battle, locked in the life and death struggle like two lions.

Meanwhile, I had made it within the city. It was pure chaos; the remaining elephants charged about in a mad frenzy, destroying homes and shops everywhere they went. I strummed a single chord on my lyre. Suddenly their destructive rampage paused. As I played and sang a merry song of hope and peace, the great beasts drew nearer to listen, to the great consternation of the Saxons.

I was not alone; the sound of Creirwy's flute harmonized with my voice, adding depth and beauty to the song. The elephants swayed to and fro to the sound. Though the Saxons whipped and beat them, the elephants simply shook them off as a dog shakes water off its fur. Enraged, the barbarians charged in to put an end to my song, but Gorlois put an end to them instead.

Meanwhile, Uther and his adversary were still locked in combat, sweating and panting from their exertions.

"You are as skilled a warrior as they say, Uther," groaned Horsa.

"Pity I cannot say the same for you, Saxon pig!"

The barbarian laughed. "And as spirited as your brother. Pity he isn't here to help you."

Uther was confused by this comment, but did not trouble himself with it. He took another swipe at the Saxon's head, which Horsa deflected with his blade, and counter-attacked with a slash to Uther's torso. The Pendragon countered Horsa's attack, but the heavy Saxon shield struck him in the face. Saxon shields are just as much an offensive weapon as defensive, and they use them as such frequently. Disoriented, Uther staggered back, his vision blurred, his ears ringing. Horsa moved in for the final attack, but Uther would not be subdued so easily. Trained in the arts of war from a young age, Uther recovered more quickly than other men. Crying out with a loud voice, Uther stepped in and took Horsa's head off with a single blow.

Their king having been defeated, deprived of their elephants and sorely beset upon by the men of Camelot, the Saxon and Pictish men were eager to retreat. They ran like rats off a sinking ship before the mighty men of Camelot, Londinium and Dyfed, scattering to the four winds.

Sheathing Caledbur, Uther looked about him, taking in the damage that the invaders had wrought. He beheld the wondrous sight of the elephants gathered peacefully about me as I played my lyre for them and smiled.

"Uther, me lad!" said King Kynyr merrily. The king of Dyfed clapped his sword-brother on the back. "You're a sight for sore eyes! Were you victorious in Hibernia?"

"Yea, verily," replied Uther. "The wolf god lies dead."

Uther paused and looked about him, anxiously. "Where is Emrys?"

Kynyr's countenance fell.

...

Nimue walked slowly down the gravel road, robed in black. Behind her walked the rest of the funeral procession. While King Emrys' remains were carried to the grave, I played my lyre and sang a lament in memory of the fallen king. At last we came to the tomb where his was to be laid.

"Man that is born of a woman hath but a short time to live, and is full of misery," said Father Dubric. "He cometh up, and is cut down, like a flower; he fleeth as it were a shadow, and never continueth in one stay."

In this manner, he continued the funeral prayers in the manner of the time. Thus King Emrys Wledig, king of Camelot, High King of Britain, was laid to rest.

After the final prayers were said, we returned to Camelot. All the way back to the great house, Nimue and Uther wept bitterly. They dismissed the men of Londinium, who had recovered the body of Vortimer, so that they might mourn him properly in their own city. Indeed, there was great lamentation in the land of Britain, for Vortimer was well-beloved by his folk.

We sat at the table as the meal was served, eating and drinking silently. Uther ate little, his hooded eyes staring straight ahead, blankly.

"He was a great king, your brother," said Kynyr. "Worthy of the title 'High King'."

"I know," said Uther as he took a draught of wine. "I have a large throne to fill."

"You'll fill it well, lad."

"I do not share your confidence, Kynyr."

"What shall you do once the child is born?" asked Creirwy.

"According to the laws," I put in, "if the child is a male, he will be eligible for his father's throne once he is of age. Until then, Uther will rule as steward."

Uther nodded in silent assent.

"And who shall train him, with no father?" asked Kynyr.

"I shall be a father to him," replied Uther. "I shall train him in the arts of battle and teach him what it means to be a good king."

Nimue nodded. "Very gracious of you, my lord."

"It is my duty," replied Uther. "I can only pray that I train him as well as his true father would have."

The lord of Camelot arose from his chair, raising his cup. "To King Emrys. May his name always be honored unto the ending of the world."

"To Emrys," replied those in the hall, before draining their cups.

Tales of the reign of Emrys faded into legend, and were forgotten by all but a few. Lack of fame, however, did by no means decrease the glory of his great deeds.

Epilogue

Elwyn took another draught of beer and spoke no further. Miss Bowen stared at him, expecting more details, but the man said nothing more.

"And then what?" she asked at last. "What happened to Nimue and the child?"

"The child – a girl – was born some months later, healthy and strong. Her name was Elysevet; a good Elvish name. Nimue returned to Avalon to be near her ailing father in his final days, and chose to raise the child among her own people."

"And what of Uther?"

"Uther was crowned High King of Britain a few days after the birth of the child."

"And what did he do after that?"

Smiling, Elwyn rose from his seat and took his coat from the rack.

"The tale of Uther's adventures is long and the hour is late. I should be heading home."

"But you will tell it one day, yes?" asked Miss Bowen.

"Of course," replied Elwyn with a wink.

Turning about, he headed out the door into the cold British night, walking down the ancient road he had walked so many times before in the centuries he had dwelt in the realm of man.